# THE SEARCH FOR
# FREEDOM

BREANNA LEE BIDDLECOMBE

WESTBOW
PRESS®
A DIVISION OF THOMAS NELSON
& ZONDERVAN

Scripture quotations taken from the New American Standard Bible®,
Copyright © 1960, 1962, 1963, 1968, 1971, 1972, 1973, 1975, 1977, 1995
by The Lockman Foundation. Used by permission. (www.Lockman.org)

WestBow Press books may be ordered through booksellers or by contacting:

WestBow Press
A Division of Thomas Nelson & Zondervan
1663 Liberty Drive
Bloomington, IN 47403
www.westbowpress.com
1 (866) 928-1240

ISBN: 978-1-5127-2559-9 (sc)
ISBN: 978-1-5127-2560-5 (e)

Library of Congress Control Number: 2015960953

Print information available on the last page.

WestBow Press rev. date: 01/20/2016

To my parents, without whom this book
would never have been published.

To Maco, I don't even know your real name, and you probably
don't remember me. Years ago you were my graceful, loving
cabin leader, to a very defiant camper. You may never know
this, but it was you who made me realize who God was.

# CHAPTER 1

CRASH!

Fredrick landed with a thud on a bag of apples that scattered across the floor. He glanced fearfully at the apples on the barn floor, then up at the slave driver who had pushed him over.

John raised an eyebrow at the sight below him and slightly shook his head in disbelief. "How did that knock you over? I barely hit you!" Before Fredrick could reply the overseer, Mr. Jenkins burst into the barn and angrily looked over at the slave laying on the floor.

"What happened?" He demanded.

"I don't know, I barely hit him and he fell onto a bunch of apples," John shrugged.

"What's wrong with you?" Mr. Jenkins demanded grabbing Fredrick's wrist and yanking him to his feet. Fredrick stumbled and managed not to fall onto the overseer before one of his steel like hands banged against Fredrick's cheek. "Can you manage to make it a whole hour without causing more trouble then you're worth?"

"Sorry," Fredrick whimpered, silently begging them not to hurt him.

Mr. Jenkins rolled his eyes and pushed on the top of the slave's head till his knees buckled, which wasn't that long. Fredrick was exhausted, malnourished, and covered with lashes and bruises. The best he could muster was kneeling on the ground panting, his unwashed, brown hair falling over his blue eyes.

"Okay..." Mr. Jenkins muttered. "You seem weaker than usual. Put the apples in the bag, bring them to the kitchen, and make sure they know they're bruised, then meet me in front of the big house, I think your Master should look at you. John, stay with him, and make sure he doesn't pass out or anything like that." With that the Overseer turned and ran out of the barn and John groaned, as if staying with Fredrick was the absolute last thing in the world he wanted to do.

Fredrick moaned and began stuffing apples back into the bag and picked them up with a grunt, almost collapsing under the weight. He shuffled them around for a few seconds before managing to shoulder them and after making the fairly long trek to the kitchen he managed to set them by the door instead of dropping them.

"What are those?" the cook, Mrs. Jenkins, the Overseer's wife, demanded.

"Apples," Fredrick answered to the floor. Most free people objected to him making eye contact. "They're bruised."

"Fine, Margret, wash and peel them, I'll figure out what I'm making with them in a few minutes." She shrugged. Fredrick glanced over at his sister who had already started collecting the apples at his feet.

It was all his fault this happened to her. The laws of Pantica stated that anyone who was caught stealing food or water should be flogged publicly, but with the odd exception, and of course, Jason was the cruel exception. Fredrick had sneaked into his kitchen to find enough to feed his homeless little sister supper, and had been caught. Since it wasn't the first time he was caught stealing from Jason, he managed to get Fredrick and Margret both forced to be slaves in his house. In other words, the perfect excuse to flog Fredrick daily and work him twice as hard, and feed him half as much as he got on the streets.

"Are you okay?" she mouthed. Fredrick shook his head and stumbled out to the porch. Mr. Jenkins stood leaning on the railing, watching Jason repeatedly slapping Margret's four year old step daughter. Fredrick was technically supposed to call him Master Cummings, but even Jason couldn't control his thoughts, as long as Fredrick kept them to himself, and in his mind, Jason wasn't worthy of the term 'Master'. That would almost imply Fredrick had any respect for him at all.

Fredrick felt an all too familiar rage bubble up inside of him at the sound of Liesel's cries. Not that he felt overly attached to her, but when you live in a one room hut with someone, who regularly begs for bedtime stories, they kind of grow on you after a while. However, he managed to suppress the rage, with his rank, as usual, if he acted wrong the whole situation would just get worse.

"Master Cummings," Fredrick announced, ignoring, with much effort, the four year old's cries. "I was told to come see you."

"I'm a little busy at the moment as you can see," Jason snapped, shoving the crying girl into the railing.

"Sorry Sir, I was just announcing my presence," Fredrick answered, using all of his strength to speak calmly. Jason groaned, grabbed Liesel's wrist, and shoved her into Fredrick's arms, who knelt down in front of her. "Go to the hut, and don't leave it until tomorrow morning, hopefully things will be calmed down by then okay?"

"Okay," she whimpered and ran off. Fredrick hesitantly stood to his feet where he was met with a slap of his own.

"Watch it, I won't use a whip on a four year old, but I won't hesitate to use one on you," Jason threatened.

"I know Sir, I'm sorry," he answered, silently thinking about how not sorry he was.

"So, he's the sick one huh?" Jason asked with a half glance behind him at the overseer. "Kill him."

"What?" Mr. Jenkins demanded. "He interrupted a four year old's beating, that's hardly reason enough to kill him!"

"Well, he's been sick for a while, and it's not the first time he's gotten involved when I'm beating another slave," Jason shrugged. "C'mere"

Fredrick stood in front of him, not daring to disobey. He crossed his skinny arms over his Grey, torn, t-shirt and stared at the sand around his feet. His feet were dirty and calloused, from years of walking barefoot, and the pants that were held up with a rag tied around his waist, were torn, patched, and faded. His skin, torn and bruised, was darkened from long hot hours under the sun.

His Master wore expensive and well-polished shoes, with high class pants wrapped around his ankles. Fredrick wasn't at all brave enough to look up past that, but he knew that everything from his balding grey head, to his pale wrinkled face, and every article of clothing he wore would've boldly shouted out how much money he had.

Jason's rough, calloused hands grabbed a fist full of his hair and pulled his head back, which caused him an instant headache. He studied his face for a while before letting his hair go, then paused for just a moment before pushing him over onto the ground.

"Hu," Jason commented as if he was the one who had just discovered something fascinating. "What time is it?"

"8:30 in the evening," Mr. Jenkins answered clearly confused.

"Yeah, let him go to bed, I'll put him out of his misery tomorrow." Jason shrugged with about as much emotion as if Fredrick was nothing more than a wounded rodent that had wondered in from the street.

"Do we have to kill him too? He's not that bad," Mr. Jenkins complained. Even John looked pretty horrified at that thought, granted, he could have been thinking if he ever got sick he'd be murdered too...

"Sir, he could get better, and he's only seventeen, a boy that age is pretty valuable," John pointed out.

"It's my slave, I can do what with him, and that goes for you too for the record," Jason answered, saying the last part with a pointed glare at John, who took half a step away from him.

"Sorry," John muttered sounding like he was more terrified then apologetic, not that Jason probably cared, he liked to keep his slaves, from drivers to kitchen drudges, terrified of him. Which wasn't that hard; Fredrick being killed was almost merciful compared to what he did when he got angry, and he was pretty easily angered.

Fredrick was scared of him too, obviously a man over you who could decide your fate with a single word, and was naturally cruel, was enough to cause fear in anyone. Mostly what he felt for his master was hatred though. Hatred for him, his wife, who was way too young for him, their annoying children who liked to throw stones at him when he was working. He hated Mr. Jenkins, who made sure he had no time to stop long enough to wipe the sweat off his forehead, his wife who did the same to his sister, the only person he let in, and John, who was like their right hand man. He had hatred for the laws of Pantica that were stacked against him, the streets he had once called a home, the hut he know lived in, and his Mother for dying before he had a chance to know her.

Jason's morals were slack, and he seemingly had no conscious. Whatever he wanted he got, no matter the cost. It didn't matter if lives were cut short or utterly destroyed. It didn't matter if children were orphaned. If you were his property, you were always at risk of being flogged for a mistake, or beaten without little sympathy. No one was fed enough. He had endless supply of wealth, and his slaves lived off of crumbs. Even the drivers, who got more food than any of the other slaves, were pretty skinny.

"My mind is made up, it's the most merciful thing to do anyway. I'll take him out to the shooting range tomorrow, and use him as target practice." Jason shrugged, jerking Fredrick back to the present. This time, not even the Overseer bothered to say anything. His fate was sealed, Fredrick would die in the morning.

\*\*\*

"Wake up," Margret's voice broke into his dreams.

"It's not morning yet," Fredrick complained voicing what his body was telling him.

5

"No, it's the middle of the night, and time for you to get up." Margret groaned. "I heard what's happening in the morning."

"Uh-huh," Fredrick answered, feverishly rolling over. "I swear, I didn't think that was going to happen. I'm so sorry, I don't wanna die! I don't wanna leave you alone."

"I know, I'll be okay, I have Markus and Liesel," Margret answered motioning to her husband and stepdaughter laying in the corner, which was kind of a lame response and Fredrick knew that. They had been forced to marry after Markus' wife was sold. They had grown into a mutual agreement, but it was kind of obvious they didn't really want to be married, since Markus already had a wife somewhere out there, and Margret was only fifteen. Fredrick sat up and wrapped his arms around his little sister, in his mind, she was his only family.

"What exactly happened?" Margret asked, she spoke quietly so as not to wake her family in the corner.

"I kind of picked the wrong time to get involved with your stepdaughter's beating," Fredrick muttered. Margret sighed and gently touched his cheek.

"You're too much like your father," She whispered.

"I'm nothing like him, I have his eyes, and I can tell stories, that's about it," Fredrick whispered back.

"No way, you're strong, gentle, you won't sit back and watch someone be wronged, and you have a massive heart. C'mon, you're too young to join our parents, and I think you can survive if given the option," Margret told him. "It's time to steal again."

"Huh?" Fredrick asked, totally confused.

"Lightning, the fastest horse in Jason's stable," Margret explained standing up. Fredrick only figured out she was talking about him running away after she peeked outside of the hut and walked out. Lightning was the Black Arabian who stayed in the stable that Fredrick had adored for years and the feeling had been mutual. His favourite chore of all time was to groom him, just so he could be with him. He wasn't allowed to ride him, but he knew how, before he had been a slave, when his father was still alive he had learned how to ride.

"Are you coming, too?" Fredrick asked after the two of them made it to the barn and he grabbed the halter and reigns hanging against the door, hoping against hope that she was.

"I can't, I have people here to take care of," Margret answered.

"But, you don't love him," Fredrick complained.

"What if I do? I don't know, Father used to say that you can never go wrong with loving someone. I don't know what I think about him. Besides, Liesel has already lost one Mother, and she's a sweetheart. I can't do that to her," Margret answered.

"You know I loved Father and adored him as much as you did, but he said a lot of things. God doesn't love us, if he did we wouldn't be doing this. Father also said that no wrong is unforgivable, well sometimes anger and bitterness is what fuels you. Some wrongs *are* unforgivable. I don't know, I have nothing against Markus, but can't you run away with me, and maybe find someone who actually loves you?"

Margret sighed, grabbed a saddle and blanket, and laid it over Lightning's back, who snorted as if to say: "where are we going at this late hour?"

"Maybe the trick isn't finding someone to love, but loving someone I've found," Margret shrugged. "I can't go, and that's that."

Fredrick sighed and helped her adjust the stirrups. "Will I ever see you again?"

"I hope so," Margret agreed. "Until then, I hope you enjoy your freedom."

"I love you," Fredrick sighed wrapping his arms around his little sister for the last time, possibly forever.

"I love you too," Margret sighed leaning into his chest. "Be sure to take the back roads, and head for the border into Markin. Travel at night, try to get as much distance from here as quickly as you can. The Oasis that Father used to take us to when we were really little, go there first and drink as much as your stomach can hold, and bring a canteen. You might not have many more opportunities to get water. Try to travel away from the road, especially when you go to sleep."

"Yes Mother," Fredrick half-heartedly teased. Margret smiled and grabbed an empty canteen from the top shelf.

"Fill this up at the oasis," she ordered. "You should go now, the gates are locked, so use the secret door behind the house."

"The one the slaves aren't supposed to know exists?" Fredrick asked only half joking before climbing into the saddle. He sighed and scratched the horse's neck, he had wanted to do this for years. Now that he finally had all he wanted to do was climb down and hug his sister again. "I'll miss you."

"I'll miss you too," Margret agreed. "But I'd rather you be alive and free then die in the morning."

"I'd rather you come with me," Fredrick sighed. "It's my fault you're a slave anyway."

"I told you before I'm proud of you, and I don't care. As for me coming with you, we all want what we can't have, now go before it's too late," Margret ordered. Fredrick sighed and dug his heels into the horse's sides. Lightning trotted out of the barn with a start, Fredrick glanced back only once, and his last view of his sister was her standing in the shadows, her shoulders shaking as if she was crying.

# CHAPTER 2

Fredrick nearly fell off Lightning's back and waded ankle deep into the oasis. He had been afraid he wouldn't be able to find it, or that it had dried up in his years of captivity, but it was there! He allowed himself a long drink and a short bath. Hoping that with all the sand and manure off of him he'd look a little different, and therefore be harder to spot. Not that it mattered. He sighed and looked at the beast casually drinking. He did steal a horse... Anyone who saw a ragged boy riding a horse would likely put two and two together.

"This whole plan is suicide!" Fredrick complained wiping the horse down with his shirt. "I'm am going to be in so much trouble! I'll be whipped till to death, or thrown into a pen of snakes, or sold to work in a cotton field or harvest sugar. What was I thinking?

"Sorry boy, that's about the best I can do. I know it's nice here, but we can't stay. We're travelling all through the night and tomorrow. C'mon, I know a way that isn't normally travelled. It's more than twice as long, but a shortcut isn't worth the risk of getting caught."

The boy and his horse road out into the sandy terrain. All night they travelled, sometimes they walked, sometimes the horse trotted. Although Fredrick would've loved to gallop the whole way he knew that wasn't even close to possible, and for Lightning's sake refused to even go into a Chanter. When the sun rose he pulled Lightning into a walk. Knowing they a limited supply of water, and he wanted to make sure that Lightning didn't get too dehydrated. When it became the hottest part of the day, he decided, they would stop and sleep, then they'd continue to travel through the rest of tomorrow night.

\*\*\*

Fredrick leaned against the horse's neck, too tired to rejoice over crossing the border. He was basically home free now that they were in Markin, but they had been running for days

Feeling bad for the horse he slipped off his back and began leading him with the reigns. The canteen of water had been emptied yesterday, and Fredrick's tongue felt like sandpaper, and stuck to the top of his mouth. His lips were chapped, but he had given up licking them a while ago, since his mouth was so dry it didn't make a difference. His head hurt and every step felt like his feet were made of lead, and it probably wasn't a good thing he didn't feel thirsty anymore.

Just when he had given up all hope he climbed a sand hill and saw a horse in the moon light. With renewed hope he stumbled over to the barn. Once inside he found a three goats, about a dozen chickens, and a camel. Lightning happily trotted over to the water trough and plunged his nose into the water. To thirsty to care that it was for the animals, and that it needed to be cleaned, Fredrick knelt by the trough and drank his fill. Then he got up, and found some grooming supplies to take care of Lightning.

After the horse was cared for Fredrick sat on a pile of hay watching him eat it, and suddenly realized how hungry he was. Back at the mansion they were only fed once in the evening, and nobody bother to feed him the last day since he was going to die anyway. In other words he hadn't eaten anything in over five days. He didn't even hesitate before grabbing a tin cup hanging from the wall, and milked the goat with a baby beside her. It was the first goat he had ever milked, but he had milked the Cummings' cow, which he figured couldn't be that different from milking the goat, and quickly filled the cup. He sat on the hay and slowly savoured the taste of the goat's milk till the cup was empty. Then he placed the cup on the floor, and refilled the canteen with water, stuffed some hay into a bag and then, using the hay to cradle them, put a couple eggs into his sack. He hesitated and grabbed the tin cup and stuffed in in the saddle bag. It would be easier to give Lightning water in the cup then from the canteen.

"I know, you don't want to travel anymore, but we can't stay here or we're going to get caught. We'll rest soon, I promise," Fredrick told him. They travelled down the road a ways, then found some tombs and Fredrick led him into them. "Alright boy, we'll spend the night here." He tied Lightning to a nook on the wall, then curled up on the ground and fell asleep. He was awoken the next morning by a black horse nuzzling his cheek. Fredrick moaned and stroked the horses face, still laying on his back.

"Good morning," Fredrick muttered. He yawned and slowly stood up. It was pretty creepy in there, various corpses lined the walls wrapped in bandages, and a long dark tunnel led down a narrow passageway.

"What do you think, Lightning? Curiosity got the better of you?" Fredrick asked. In answer Lightning pulled against the lead rope towards the hay. "I take it horses are more interested in breakfast then adventures?" Lightning tugged on the lead rope a little more and Fredrick sighed. "Alright, you can have a small breakfast. We do need to ration our food, and then, we'll go down the tunnel? I'm not going out there in broad daylight, and I don't want to stay here all day."

While Lightning chewed his handful of hay Fredrick had a small sip of water from the canteen, then poured a little water into the cup and offered it to Lightning who drank it greedily. "Now let's go! C'mon, I'm totally free, with literally no one to tell me what to do. If I want to go down the tunnel, because I want to go down the tunnel, I'm gonna go down the tunnel."

He walked down into the tunnel, leading the horse behind him. Pretty much nothing new till he climbed out on the other side, with dry, yellow grass and various thistles blanketing the new ground, but he was satisfied, after doing something just because he wanted to. The sun was setting, and the sky was orange, and various clouds were a florescent pink.

"Who knew we were walking so long, huh boy?" he asked. He glanced behind them a ways and saw another farm house. Fredrick shrugged and placed the rest of the hay down at Lightning's front hooves. "You mine as well eat it. I'll probably be able to find you some more food in there."

Fredrick examined his eggs, deciding how he was going to eat them. He sat down on the grass and cracked one open, carefully keeping the egg in half the eggshell, then poured it into his mouth. "You know if you get past the slime it's not that bad," He shrugged. The horse's snort almost sounded like a laugh.

"You're mocking me, aren't you?" Fredrick teased scratching Lightning behind the ear. He drank some of the water from the canteen, and poured the rest into the cup for Lightning.

Fredrick sat in the grass, watching the house in the distance. Once he saw someone go into the barn, and then after a pause walk back out into the farm house Fredrick mounted Lightning and galloped into the barn.

Four cows, one camel, and two horses stood in various stalls on one side of the barn, and about a dozen chickens sat along a row on the other side. He quickly refilled the canteen, and then began scooping grain into the bag, planning to arrange them so the eggs weren't touching after he was long gone. Just then the door opened, and Fredrick quickly dove behind the barrel of grain.

"Come out, I know you're in here," a male voice announced after a pause. "Either that or I suddenly have a horse I didn't know I owned." Fredrick didn't move, but sat, paralysed with fear. In a few seconds a middle aged man stood in front of him, He had Gray hair, and a receding forehead. A light tan covered his strong arms and calloused hands. He wore worn shoes, although in better shape than John's shoes had been, his pants, which were held up with suspenders, looked as if they had been mended and patched several times. His face was unreadable.

"Well, well, well, what do we have here? A runaway slave who's stolen his master's horse, and now tries to steal my grain?" he asked, not sounding accusing or judgemental, more like he was making an innocent observation.

Fredrick blinked momentarily, shocked at how quickly he figured that out. "No!"

"No?" He laughed. "What part do you deny? Your bag leads a trail of grain to my barrel, you dress in rags and bare feet, and have a horse in your possession. Either you're a homeless beggar with such high class mean of travel as a horse, or you're a runaway slave, with your master's horse. And I haven't even mentioned the scars on your back, which again, points to the obvious answer of 'runaway'."

"Please don't turn me in," Fredrick whispered. "I'm sorry, I'll give the grain back, and I just can't go back to my Master."

The man sighed and knelt in front of him. "Do you know how much trouble I could get in for helping a runaway?"

"You don't have to help me, please, just let me go!" Fredrick begged. "My master wants to kill me!"

"Tell you what, I'm not going to turn you in. I am going to make you give the grain back however, and if you do that, I think my wife still has some leftover supper you can eat, and we can get your horse taken care of."

Fredrick glanced up in confusion, surely this must be some kind of mistake. No one freely gave food away to thieves, but three years a slave had taught him to do what he was told, when he was told, with no questions asked. The man never once took his eyes off of him as he unloaded the grain back into the barrel, when Fredrick reached to bottom of his sack, and the man saw the eggs his expression didn't even change.

"I know you didn't get those from this farm, my son just came in here and collected all my eggs. Where did they come from?" he asked.

"A farm down yonder. I couldn't show you the way above land, I travelled through the catacombs all day. And it wasn't like I took all the eggs, only some of them," Fredrick answered, adding the last part as a defence.

"What about the rest of your stuff? Did that come from your Master or somewhere else?" he asked.

"I got a tin cup from the same place, the rest of it came from my master's," Fredrick muttered.

"How long has your journey been?" the man asked, still totally emotionless.

"I ran away five days ago," he answered looking at the floor. He thought about pouring the water back into the trough, but surely the man would lose the temper he must be holding back after that. "It's a seven day journey. Mostly we travelled at night, and sometimes during the day, especially after we crossed the border."

"Your poor horse!" the man exclaimed and Fredrick ducked almost out of habit at the sharp tone. "Your horse needs rest, you know?"

"Sorry," Fredrick muttered.

"Don't apologize to me." The man sighed. "So, are you running to anything particular, or are you just running away?"

"I was just running away, really... I knew I wanted to leave Pantica, and I already did that, so I don't know where I'm going to now," Fredrick muttered.

"Well you can stay here till you make up your mind," the man sighed, and added in a softer tone. "I'm not going to hurt you, I promise. Although, just so you know, you're free now, and free men look each other in the eyes." Fredrick slowly looked up at him and made eye contact, long enough to see that he had blue eyes, that were highlighted by various laugh and tired lines, before lowering his eyes again.

"Well, it's a start." The man sighed, then extended his hand in greeting. "I'm Mathew Couring, what's your name?" For a brief moment Fredrick stared at the hand, trying to remember when the last time someone had offered to shake his hand was before grabbing it.

"Fredrick," he mumbled.

"Well Fredrick, it seems like you've had quite the adventure so far. C'mon, let's go get you something to eat," the man, Mathew, commented, motioning towards the door.

"I'm okay, I can just move on from here," Fredrick muttered taking half a step away from him. Mathew walked over and raised the boy's chin so Fredrick, who wasn't putting up much of a fight anyway, was forced to look into his eyes.

"I'm not about to let a half starved boy 'move on from here' with no food for himself, or his horse, and very little, if any, water. Come on, I insist you eat something," Mathew told him.

Feeling compelled to obey, Fredrick nodded slowly. "Okay, let's go." Mathew led the way into the house, with Fredrick trailing behind him. The first room they walked into was a kitchen. A long table, with various chairs sat on one side, and a hearth, that had been swept clean, stood just across from it. He had hardly stepped into the room when a middle aged woman with fading blonde hair and brown eyes, that Fredrick assumed was Mathew's wife, suddenly stood right in front of him.

"Goodness child, look at you, you're near skin and bones! Elizabeth, fetch him some leftovers from supper, make sure to include a large helping of meat," she exclaimed playing with his to long hair. "Come here honey, sit at the table."

"Aaron, his horse is in the barn, why don't you go take care of it," Mathew ordered as a girl about Margret's age began preparing a plate of food. A boy, about a year or two younger, got up and walked out the door. "Girls, don't stare at him, give the boy some privacy and head up to your room."

Fredrick watched out of the corner of his eye as a little girl, and another one probably just short of a preteen, reluctantly ran out of the room. He was half aware of himself sitting down at the table, but it felt weird to be waited on.

"Here you are," the girl, Mathew's wife had called Elizabeth, said while placing a plate full of food in front of her. Fredrick glanced up at her, making eye contact with her, that wasn't as hard as the other two, since she reminded him so much or Margret. As soon as he looked at her he glanced down at the floor.

"Thanks," he answered quickly, afraid to look at her face again, that evidently looked a lot more like Margret then he had bargained for. Her eyes were smaller, she was maybe a few inches taller, she was a healthy weight, and much cleaner, but it was Margret's face in Elizabeth's. Their heads were the same shape, and their eyes were the same shape, the hair colour was almost the same.

He glanced down at his food and blinked. There was a piece of steak that took up nearly half of his plate, some mashed potatoes and boiled beans filled the rest of it. Before he had totally registered what he all had Elizabeth had placed a cup full of milk and some cutlery in front of his plate. "Is all that for me?"

"Yes honey, it's all for you," the woman told him gently. "Go on, eat up." Fredrick picked up the cutlery, and cut a piece of the meat off, feeling self-conscious with everyone just watching him.

"So..." Fredrick muttered trying to make conversation, holding the meat on his fork. "So" was pretty much all he said though, after years of being told to speak when spoken to, and being flogged if he spoke out of turn, he was pretty bad at making conversation. Mathew picked up on what he was trying to do and started a conversation between his wife and daughter. As soon as Fredrick stuffed the streak into his mouth he realized he hadn't eaten meat in years, and it exploded with a flavour he had long forgotten. Finding he was way hungrier than he had originally assumed he almost couldn't stuff the steak into his mouth fast enough. The potatoes and beans were flavours forgotten too, since he normally only ever ate his vegetables raw.

"If you're as hungry as you look, and you eat that fast you're going to throw it up, slow down, and chew your food. It's not going anywhere," Elizabeth told him, grabbing his wrist and holding it so the fork couldn't reach his mouth.

"Okay." Fredrick nodded, after a pause and he realized Elizabeth wanted a reply. She dropped his wrist and Fredrick continued to eat, although at a slower pace.

"That's a nice horse out there," the other boy, Aaron, announced coming in. "Arabian right? What's his name?"

"Lightning," Fredrick answered with a mouthful of food, he swallowed and glanced over at Aaron, who had light brown hair, blue eyes, and a medium tan.

"Yeah, he's a good horse," Aaron nodded. "What's your name?"

"Fredrick," he answered half wishing everybody would stop talking to him so he could eat, not that he was close to brave enough to actually say that out loud.

"I'm Aaron." He shrugged, looking down at Fredrick's now half empty plate. He had large hazel eyes, and messy brown hair with a thick tan, and Fredrick guessed he was probably fourteen or fifteen.

"I'm Elizabeth," Margret's lookalike offered. "My Mother's name is Victoria, and I assume you exchanged names with my Father in the barn."

"Yes Ma'am." Fredrick nodded.

"Elizabeth, please," she begged.

"Elizabeth," Fredrick repeated, trying it out. Silence again and Fredrick greedily ate the rest of the food.

"Do you want more?" Elizabeth asked when he scraped the rest of the mashed potatoes and onto his fork and ate them.

"No, I'm okay, thank-you," Fredrick answered.

"Really?" Mathew asked and Fredrick half laughed.

"Yeah, I'm okay, that was more food than I've eaten at one time in years, if ever, actually that was a lot of meat," he answered. "It was delicious, thank you."

"Oh, don't even mention it," Victoria told him as he picked up his cup and plate.

"I'll take that, don't worry about it," Elizabeth offered, taking the plate from him. "You just sit down and relax." Fredrick obeyed, and his hands unused to sitting idle began to subconsciously drum on the table.

# CHAPTER 3

"If I stay, I'll be a major threat to your entire family," Fredrick replied to Victoria's suggestion to stay. Elizabeth had gone upstairs to play with her little sisters, and Aaron was supposedly reading in his room.

"Do you want to stay?" Mathew asked. Fredrick hesitated then shook his head.

"You've been so kind to me, I don't want to put you at risk," Fredrick answered.

"Please, just stay for a few nights, you're so malnourished I'm afraid if you leave you'll die before you reach the next town," Victoria told him.

"I doubt your master will come looking this far from the border anyway. It'll be more of an inconvenience then a profit anyway."

"Lightning's a really good horse," Fredrick contradicted.

"I still don't think he'll travel this far," Mathew shrugged. "But we do have ways of hiding you both."

"There's an extra bed in the barn," Victoria explained. "Mathew and Aaron can bring it in, Aaron hates having a room to himself anyway."

"I'm fine," Fredrick replied. "I don't want to be any trouble. I always sleep on the floor. I really don't need anything."

"Nonsense, you're our guest, and we're not about to just let you sleep on the floor when there is an available bed for you, in the very

19

least you'd share a bed with Aaron," Victoria told him. "And Mathew can bring in the washtub, there's an oasis just over the hill, so you can have a bath and clean off. You're going to have to get back into the clothes you have now though, I'll see to making new ones for you tomorrow."

"Why?" Fredrick demanded. "I tried to rob you!"

"Well, you gave it back," Mathew shrugged.

"After you caught me, and told me to! I would've left with your grain, and you never would've heard from me again! I'm sorry? What do you want from me?" Fredrick almost yelled, which surprised him because he hadn't yelled since he was like, seven.

"Nothing," Victoria answered simply.

"Do you realize how little sense that makes?" Fredrick asked keeping his voice down this time.

"Fredrick, has anyone ever told you stories from the bible?" Mathew asked.

"What?" Fredrick asked, totally confused. "Yeah, my father used to tell them to me and my sister before we would go to bed. How does that even connect though? He was the only decent person I ever met that believed them. The rest were all murderers and thieves who rip people's backs to shreds for making eye contact, or not agreeing with everything they say, or speaking when they're not spoken too. I was orphaned on the street 'cause my father, who wouldn't hurt a fly, was cheated out of everything he owned by Christians and died of starvation. I was sold into slavery for trying to steal enough food to feed my little sister."

"Do I look like a murderer, or a thief? And I can promise you, I don't even own a whip," Mathew told him as Victoria gently rested her hand on Fredrick's. Fredrick wasn't even sure how to respond to the touch, he was almost certain he could count on one hand the number of people who had touched his hand that softly, and have fingers left over, yet it was strangely soothing.

"Well, I didn't mean you were a thief and murderer..." Fredrick muttered, staring at Victoria's hand a moment longer before looking up at Mathew again.

"I know, but you do make a point, and I won't deny that there are hypocrites out there," Mathew answered. "I will, however, deny that that is what Christianity is about, 'cause it's not. It's about loving your neighbour, doing good to those who do evil, praying for those who rise up against you, forgiving those who do you wrong cause ultimately that's what Christ did for us. Romans 5:8 'But God demonstrates his own love toward us, in that while we were yet sinners, Christ died for us.' Christianity is about learning to love others, even those, especially those, who don't deserve it."

"Well that's... heavy..." Fredrick blinked. "I've never even heard that before. Isn't that, like, letting people just get away with doing wrong? What happened to justice?"

"There is such thing as tough love, and letting people get away with whatever they want is sometimes the least loving thing you can do. Granted, that may be the Father of six coming out in me, but even among other people, 'Never take your own revenge, beloved, but leave room for the wrath of God, for it is written, 'vengeance is Mine, I will repay,' says the Lord,' Romans 12:19. God is a God of justice, and though it may seem like the wicked prosper, and those that do evil have everything good thrown at them, but think about it. What good is any of that after they die? They're doomed to Hell, where there *will* be weeping, and gnashing of teeth," Mathew answered.

"What good is *anything* after you die?" Fredrick asked.

"I beg to differ, the bible talks about treasures stored up in heaven, those come by loving others, not just those that love you, everybody does that, but loving those who hate you. Not because you're obligated, but because you recognize that Jesus loved us when we didn't deserve it, and the least we can do is to show that kind of love to others," Mathew answered.

"But... how do you do that when... when..." Fredrick began, then stopped, unsure how to word what he wanted to say.

"You ask Jesus for help, nobody can do that kind of thing on their own strength, sometimes, loving your enemies is so hard you have to start with praying for the strength to just pray for them, other times it's way easier. The most important step of all, is realizing that carrying around that much anger is more exhausting to you, and causes more damage to you, then it ever will to them."

"That still sounds hard," Fredrick complained.

"That's 'cause it is, but it's worth it." Mathew smiled. There was silence for a while before Victoria stood up.

"Goodness, it's late, those girls are going to be half asleep tomorrow if we don't get them in bed right now, and Aaron's hard enough to get up when he goes to bed on time!"

"Laura! Ethel! Aaron!" Mathew yelled to the ceiling. In a few seconds two girls, one about 8 with dirty blonde hair, the other about 10 with brown hair, both with freckles, strait noses, blue eyes, and two braids running down their backs, appeared in the door, followed by Aaron. "This is Fredrick, he may or may not be staying with us." Pointing to the blonde, he added to Fredrick. "That's Laura, our youngest, and this is Ethel. It's time to get ready for bed."

The two girls flew into the room and into their Father's open arms. "Can we have a story?" Laura asked looking up at him.

"Not tonight, it's too late, tomorrow I'll tell you one okay?" Mathew answered.

"You said that yesterday," Ethel bargained.

"No, I said *maybe* yesterday, tomorrow I will," Mathew contradicted. "Go on, wash your face, comb your hair, and get your nightclothes on."

"Okay, I love you Pa," Ethel answered hugging him around his neck.

"Love you too," Mathew answered hugging both girls and kissing their foreheads. "Love you Laura."

"I love you too!" She smiled, then both of them turned and darted out the doorway, past their sister that Fredrick hadn't even seen come in.

"Okay, make your decision now Fredrick," Mathew ordered, and Fredrick immediately panicked, unsure what he wasn't sure what to do, but stood up anyway.

"I'll uh... I'll spend the night, it beats the streets," He announced quickly.

"Alright, Aaron, come on and help me bring the bed in the barn up to your room, then it's time for bed," Mathew announced standing up. "Elizabeth, can you pull out some extra bedding and make the bed once we get it in?"

"Yes Pa," Elizabeth answered, leaving the room through the same way she had come.

"I can help," Fredrick offered.

"I'm a little worried you'll pass out if you do," Mathew told him honestly. "Victoria, maybe you should get him some water, his lips are pretty chapped."

\*\*\*

Fredrick was back at Jason's mansion, except there was no one there. Somehow it seemed more frightening now than it ever had in the past. Fredrick slowly started walking aimlessly, his feet feeling like hundred pound weights.

"Margret?" he called out, almost without thinking, his voice coming out louder then he meant it too.

"*Breathe!*" he told himself mentally. "*You're panicking!*"

"Margret!" he called, this time in a whisper. Then fell to the ground and started sobbing. That's when Jason grabbed Fredrick's arm before he even saw him coming and Fredrick screamed and jumped up.

"Sorry," Aaron gasped backing up across the room and pressing himself against the wall next to the trunk full of clothes at the end of his bed. Fredrick stood in front of his own bed, panting and sweating.

"Is everyone okay?" Mathew demanded running into the room, from the door that was at the foot of Fredrick's bed. Immediately Fredrick gasped in fear and pressed himself against the wall.

"He was crying in his sleep, I woke him up and he screamed," Aaron answered still standing against the wall.

"Fredrick, you need to breathe, everything's okay," Mathew ordered. Fredrick nodded, feeling cold outside of the blankets, but mostly terrified. Who knew what he'd would be like after waking up in the middle of night, and having his children woken up? A week without being beaten, which was probably a three year long record for him, now over.

"Okay seriously Fredrick, you're going make yourself pass out," Mathew told him sounding even sterner. Fredrick forcibly let out a few shaky breaths and leaned against the wall, still shaking with fear. "Okay, are you guys ready to tell me what happened?"

"I don't know, I already told you, he was crying in his sleep so I grabbed his shoulder, he screamed, and here we are," Aaron explained.

"Okay, Fredrick, it was just a dream," Mathew told him plainly. He started to walk towards him, when Fredrick whimpered and sank to the ground, raising his arms to protect his face from Mathew's fists. "Aaron, go get your Mother." Aaron obeyed and darted out of the room, while Mathew stood a few feet away from him, clearly at a loss for what to do.

"What?" Victoria asked coming in and wrapping her house coat around her nightclothes, with Aaron trailing behind her.

"He's terrified, and panics every time I come near him," Mathew answered holding out his hand to motion to him.

"Okay sweetie, it's okay, no one is gonna hurt you here, you're safe," Victoria told him gently walking slowly towards him, as if approaching a frightened animal. She slowly knelt down and extended her hand, with Fredrick watching her every movement, and rested it on his knee. "You're okay honey, don't worry, no one is going to hurt you, Mathew included." She half glanced back at her husband and motioned for him to join them. He walked over in roughly the same way Victoria had and sat beside Fredrick with his back to the wall.

"Your arms are covered in bruises, I don't know how I missed that last night," Victoria commented examining them. She used a really soft voice, and sounded like she was just trying to come up with stuff to talk about, but Fredrick slowly started to relax, listening the older woman talk. "Are they from blocking blows to your face? Probably huh? You're really brave to run away. I know you're scared, and honestly I'd be scared too, but it's okay. He's in a different country. No one is going to hurt you here."

"It was just a dream," Mathew repeated, softer this time, like someone would talk to a frightened little kid.

"No it wasn't, my master wanted to kill me," Fredrick told them as humiliating tears squeezed out of his eyes. "And I'm never going to see my sister again! What was I thinking? I'm gonna be whipped till there isn't any skin left on my back!"

Across the room Aaron opened his mouth as if to say something but must've thought better of it because he closed his mouth.

"Okay, I promise, I will do everything in my power to stop them from doing that. You're never going to be a slave again if I have anything to say about the matter alright?" Mathew promised.

"If they find me you won't," Fredrick argued.

"That's why I'm not going to let them find you," Mathew promised.

"I don't wanna be whipped again, I want my Father, and I want my sister, but one's dead and the other one I abandoned!" Fredrick complained beginning to shiver again, but more from cold then fear this time.

Victoria and Mathew made eye contact and seemingly had a mental conversation. There expressions almost looked pained.

"I'm sure she's happy you're free now," Victoria told him finally.

"Of course she is, she was the one who told me to run away. Margret's still a slave though, and our master is so cruel," Fredrick told him. "What if he finds out she helped me runaway?"

"What if he doesn't?" Mathew asked gently, to which Fredrick just sighed and rested his forehead on his knees, one of which still had Victoria's hand resting on them.

"Sweetheart, you should go back to bed, you're burning up," Victoria told him as soon as his forehead touched her hand.

Fredrick nodded, not really moving, "I've been sick for a while, when I wasn't seeming to get better my master decided that it would be best to just shoot me. He was going to do that the morning after I ran away."

The two looked at each other, and had another mental conversation. Mathew gently rested his hand on one of Fredrick's shoulders. "No one is gonna hurt you here," He promised again. Other than that no one said anything, until Fredrick's panic attack was officially over and he started to feel exhausted.

"Okay, you ready to go back to sleep?"

"Okay." Fredrick nodded.

"Alright, I'm not going to let them find you alright?" Mathew promised as Fredrick climbed onto the bed again. "Aaron, if you're ever brave enough to wake him up again, you would probably be wise not to grab him."

"Okay," Aaron answered, still not moving from the spot where he stood when he first came in.

"Okay, both of you, try to go back to sleep," Mathew ordered standing up, and the two of them obeyed without objections. Mathew sighed and walked down the hall to the room his daughters shared and peeked into the door.

"You okay Lizzie?" he asked.

"What happened?" she whispered sitting up.

"Your brother woke our guest up from a nightmare by grabbing his arm, everything's okay now though, but that boy needs a lot of love, I'll tell you about it in the morning. Did the girls wake up?" he whispered.

"Ethel did, but I think she went back to sleep," Elizabeth answered.

"Okay, everything's alright, I just came in to see if you were okay. Just try and go back to sleep," He whispered to her. She obeyed and laid back down. Mathew walked back to his own bedroom and lay down next to his wife, who immediately sat up and looked at him.

"Why is he even here?" Victoria asked. "Hasn't this family gone through enough? Why couldn't you just feed him and send him on his way, does it have to be this big thing?"

"Matt," Mathew sighed. "He looked at me, and I saw Matt."

"Mathew, I can't lose you, and I certainly can't have that boy sleeping in there in Matt's bed," Victoria told him, nearly in tears. Mathew sighed again and wrapped his arms around her. His bride, the girl he vowed to take care of forever nearly twenty five years ago. He had no idea there would come a day when he wasn't sure how to take care of himself, let alone Victoria.

"I think we need him," Mathew told her. "As much as that frightened and abused orphan in there needs us, I think we need him more. Somehow, we need to learn that there's still life out there."

"He's not Matt, and he's not Johnny..." Victoria began, then started crying into his chest. "I miss them so much, I can't handle this."

"I know," he whispered. "I miss them too." He laid awake hugging her for a long time, but even after she fell asleep he still stayed awake, staring into the darkness. Somehow, he knew that Fredrick was never going to replace them, but he needed him. If only for the reason that for the first time in months, he couldn't search all night. He was compelled to stay in bed, and look out for the part of his family he could still look out for, and Fredrick.

# CHAPTER 4

Mathew may have told Fredrick to go back to sleep, but he didn't. He lay awake for hours, watching images of the Jenkins accuse Margret of helping him, John was looking for him, and Jason... just the sight of him was enough to cause fear. Finally in an effort to distract his mind he sat up, with his back to the wall, tearing the fingernails off his fingers till they were pretty much all gone. When the first light of dawn came Fredrick stood up. Aaron was still sleeping so he quietly made the bed and went downstairs.

The first room you walked into once you made it down the steep stairs was a sitting room, a fireplace sat in the corner and around it were a handful of chairs, next to one of the chairs was a table with candles on top of it, and drawer underneath. A coil rug that Fredrick assumed was handmade blanketed the floor. Nobody seemed to be up down here either, but in a few minutes, creaks coming from upstairs suggested that was changing.

Fredrick glanced at various chairs around the sitting room, but sat on the ground. He had nothing better to do anyway. About a minute later Mathew came down stairs and Fredrick jumped to his feet and stared at his feet.

"Good morning Fredrick," Mathew greeted glancing over at him. "How long have you been awake?"

"A few minutes," Fredrick lied. "I wasn't sure what I was supposed to do."

"Stay indoors for now," Mathew told him. "I'll take care of your horse. Lightning right? If you want a morning chore though, you can wake up my insomniac son, Aaron. It's probably the hardest one around here. I already woke him up, but you'll have to wake him up again in a couple minutes, he usually goes back to sleep."

"Sure." Fredrick smiled for only a moment before his smile fell again. "Sorry about last night."

"You don't have to say sorry for getting scared here," Matthew told him. "Do you have nightmares a lot?"

"Yeah," Fredrick sighed staring at the wall. "I've been having them almost every night ever since my Father was robbed when I was nine, since not a whole lot of good things have happened since then, I don't easily run out of things to dream about."

"Well, maybe someday they'll go away again," Mathew comforted. "I'm going to head out to the barn. Aaron will be asleep again by now."

"What kind of insomniac falls asleep that fast?" Fredrick asked hesitantly.

"The first time he goes to sleep it usually takes him a few hours, then he's out, and it's nearly impossible to get him up. He's had a pretty hard year, this insomnia thing just came up recently. As near as we've been able to figure out, once he sits up, he's actually awake. Don't worry about going easy on him though, anything that will get him out of bed, do it," Mathew told him. "And... he may threaten to, but he's not actually going to hurt you. Once he sits up he's usually actually up. If you don't want to, you don't have to."

"I'm good," Fredrick answered. "I'll do it."

"Aaron," he announced walking into the room a few minutes later. Sure enough, he had fallen back asleep. "Rise and shine." Aaron either didn't wake up, or ignored him. Fredrick hesitantly walked up poked his shoulder, to which Aaron responded to by snarling at him.

"Aaron, your Father said it's time to get up, he wants you to help him in the barn," Fredrick told him.

"How nice for him," Aaron groaned, his eyes still closed. Since Fredrick wasn't sure how to respond to that he grabbed him some work clothes from the trunk, and tossed them at his head. When he didn't move Fredrick stood by the foot of the bed studying him.

*And so the fight begins...* he thought.

After Aaron finally made it to the barn, after a battle of wills, still grumbling about it being way to early and how he was to tired, Fredrick strolled towards the kitchen and stood in the doorway till Elizabeth looked up from stirring something, that looked almost like paste.

"Good morning," she greeted. "You can come in."

"Good morning," he greeted.

"Good morning," the brunette girl, Ethel, greeted. Her blue eyes, unlike her brother's, looked refreshed from a good night's sleep, and they danced with delight.

"Good morning." He grinned. "You look ready to tackle the day."

"Yep, I'm a morning person," Ethel grinned.

"I can tell, it's nice to know someone in this family is," Fredrick commented.

"Did my pa make you wake up Aaron?" Elizabeth asked.

"Well, he wouldn't let me go outside, and I need something to do in the morning." Fredrick shrugged.

"I guess," Elizabeth agreed thoughtfully. Ethel just shook her head like she couldn't believe he had to wake him up.

"You still look feverish," Elizabeth commented.

"I'm feeling better," Fredrick shrugged. Elizabeth shrugged and dumped some of the paste stuff onto a grill with a spoon.

"Hey, you're making pancakes," Fredrick pointed out, Elizabeth smiled and looked up at him.

"Yeah, I'm making pancakes, what did you think it was?" she asked.

"I had no idea." Fredrick shrugged as Laura came in.

"Good morning," she muttered her blonde hair falling in a tangled mess down her back.

"Good morning Laura, don't you remember our deal? I'll braid your hair for you, but you have to brush it," Elizabeth greeted.

"Can't you brush it Lizzie?" Laura sighed.

"Nope, I've gotta finish breakfast," Elizabeth answered.

"I can do it," Ethel offered.

"No, you've gotta go get the water from the oasis," Elizabeth told her. "You should actually go do that now before breakfast is ready."

"Alright." Ethel shrugged, running out of the house.

"Where's your Ma?" Fredrick asked suddenly realizing that Elizabeth and Ethel were doing everything themselves.

"She usually sleeps in," Elizabeth answered like there was more to that story, but she didn't want to share it…Suddenly Fredrick was left wondering what happened in the past year.

"I can brush your hair Laura, come on, where's your hair brush?" Fredrick offered. Laura's eyes lit up, and something told Fredrick that she didn't usually get an opportunity to be treated like a little girl.

It took until Victoria came downstairs but Fredrick managed to yank all the tangles out of Laura's hair with her only saying "ow" a handful of times so he figured he probably did a pretty good job. He had practice on Liesel's hair.

"Fredrick, if you wanna wash up for breakfast it will be in a few minutes," Elizabeth offered quickly french braiding her sister's hair.

"Um, where do I wash up?" he asked.

"Just in the bucket I just brought in," Ethel answered sitting at the table. Fredrick nodded and knelt down by a pail, picked up the bar of soap, and stared at it, suddenly realizing he hadn't held a bar of soap ever, in his life. He rolled it over in his hand for a while, completely unsure how to use it.

Fortunately Mathew came in a moment later, and saw Fredrick in the corner examining the soap. Without saying a word he knelt in front of him, took the bar of soap from him, washed his hands, and gave it back to him.

"Thank you," Fredrick whispered, washing his own hands with it. Mathew gently clutched Fredrick's head, stood up and hugged his daughter.

"Good morning Elizabeth," he greeted.

"Morning Pa," She smiled scraping the eggs that she had scrambled and cooked into a bowl as Aaron walked into the house and Good Mornings were exchanged among the Courings. By the time the food was at the table and they were all sitting down Fredrick was standing awkwardly in the corner.

"C'mon Fredrick, sit at the table," Mathew offered, and Fredrick obeyed suddenly aware that he was staring at the food with his mouth half open. There was just so much of it!

As soon as he sat down everyone simultaneously bowed their heads, but Fredrick glanced around for a second before following their lead. Mathew led them in a prayer which, in Fredrick's opinion, took forever. Mathew had to pretty much thank God for everything, his family being together, their health, the food, "...And Lord, thank you for bringing Fredrick here safely, we pray that you will keep him safe and hidden, and strength on his road to healing. In your name, Amen."

"So, how long are you planning on staying?" Mathew asked. "You're welcome as long as you want to."

"Okay, if you really want me to I can stay," Fredrick answered. Even if there was no possible way they really loved him the way they said they did, last night had convinced him that maybe they wouldn't beat him for the slightest error.

*And besides, there is no way I can starve here...* he thought to himself as Elizabeth put two full pancakes on his plate, and then started dishing him eggs.

"I'm good," Fredrick objected holding his hands out to stop her from putting on a third scoop of eggs on his plate.

"Are you sure?" Elizabeth asked.

"I can go for seconds, if need be." Fredrick laughed. Honestly, he was pretty sure no one had ever tried to give him too much food before.

"If Fredrick's staying here, what are we going to do about tonight?" Elizabeth asked.

"I was just thinking about that, Fredrick, you're going to have to stay in your room upstairs," Mathew answered.

"What's going on tonight?" Fredrick asked looking up at his face.

"My oldest, Andrew, his pregnant wife Martha, and their little girl are coming over for supper," Mathew answered.

"Couldn't we just cancel?" Aaron asked.

"It's too late for that, if we do that now they're bound to ask questions, Fredrick is just going to have to hide," Mathew answered.

"Why does he have to hide?" Laura asked.

"It's a long story, I'll tell you when you're older," Mathew explained. "You two can't tell your brother about him, understood?" Laura and Ethel both nodded simultaneously.

"What about Lightning? Hiding a skinny teenager's one thing, hiding a horse is something totally different," Aaron pointed out.

"We'll see what we can do, 'And who of you by being worried can add a single hour to his life?'" Mathew answered.

"My Father used to say that," Fredrick exclaimed in surprise.

"It's a quote from the bible, Mathew 6:27, Jesus said it first." Mathew smiled.

"Interesting." Fredrick nodded.

"I'm not too concerned," Mathew continued. "Even if Andrew finds either of them it's likely it'll all work out. He was raised with the same morals instilled into him as you."

"So was Matt," Aaron muttered stabbing his food.

"Who?" Fredrick asked.

"My second oldest," Mathew explained with a hint of an edge to his voice. "Anyway, Fredrick I want you to stay close to the house,

I'm sure Victoria can find something for you to do if you're bored, but I want you to avoid going outside."

"Okay," Fredrick muttered stuffing part of a pancake into his mouth.

After breakfast Mathew and Aaron went to work in the fields, Ethel and Laura began doing dishes, and Victoria decided that Fredrick needed a new outfit so she pulled out some yarn and measured Fredrick with it. He stood in the living room, watching her sew for a while till Margret's look alike came in and stood in the door.

"I'm going for a walk," Victoria announced setting her sewing aside and standing up, which seemed kind of random to Fredrick since she had just been sewing a moment before but he seemed to be the only one who noticed that. "Elizabeth why don't you make a dinner stew?

"Alright." Elizabeth shrugged before walking into the kitchen again. Fredrick glanced at Victoria again and then followed Margret's lookalike.

As Fredrick got to know her though he learned that even though she was like Margret's mirror image, she acted nothing like her. Even when they were free, little kids without a care in the world, Margret was pretty quiet, shy, and rarely spoke around someone she hardly knew. Elizabeth went about her cooking, talking to Fredrick like they had known each other their whole lives. It was nice to be talked to like an equal by someone besides his usual three people.

"Are you bored?" Elizabeth asked looking up from cutting carrots after a while.

"Um... sort of, my hands are bored, but I'm enjoying talking to you," Fredrick answered. Elizabeth looked up at him and smiled in an amused way.

"Well, if your hands need something to do you can always shell some peas," Elizabeth suggested.

"Gladly," Fredrick agreed wondering over to a pile of peas and cracking one open. "How many do you want?"

"Fill this bowl about half full with peas," Elizabeth answered handing him a salad bowl.

"How old are you?" Fredrick asked beginning to shell the peas.

"I'm fifteen," She answered. "Aaron's 12, Ethel's 9, and Laura's 7."

"Aaron's only 12?" Fredrick demanded looking up, though his hands didn't cease to work. "That kid is tall!"

"Yeah, he is tall, it's pretty crazy," Elizabeth answered. "My older brothers did that too, and apparently my Father did, they like shoot up, and then are done growing by like fourteen or fifteen. However, once you get to know him he acts like he's twelve, so it works out."

"Yeah, I guess he's pretty immature, but yeah, he can very well be done growing in a couple years, either that or he's gonna be like a giant," Fredrick agreed.

"Yeah, one or the other." Elizabeth laughed.

# CHAPTER 5

Fredrick lay in bed, wrapped in quilts, silently wondering if he'd ever feel warm again. The Courings had sent him upstairs a while ago before Andrew showed up with his family. He had pretty much been up here ever since, half dozing, half staring into space.

That's when a guy, he assumed was Andrew, burst into the room. Fredrick jumped to his feet, feeling dizzy from getting up so fast, and for a moment everything went black. He panicked for a moment thinking he was going to pass out, which had been happening more and more lately, but fortunately he recovered before then. When his vision cleared the man who stood in front of him was about six feet, strong, tanned, with dirty blonde hair in need of a cut, and blue eyes.

"Sit down kid, you look like you're gonna pass out," he ordered as Mathew and Victoria walked in behind him. Fredrick glanced at them for just a moment then slowly sat down with his back sliding against the wall. "Okay, I guess you're allowed to hide that... When did he show up?"

"Yesterday evening," Mathew sighed.

"And what's in the barn?"

"A horse."

"So you have a runaway slave in your house, and I'm guessing that's a stolen horse in the barn, and you're sure you're not going to get into trouble with the law?" Andrew asked.

"I can leave," Fredrick offered.

"No, you're not leaving, you still have a fever, and you're malnourished," Mathew ordered. Fredrick cringed half expecting a blow to come with the harsh tone but Mathew only sighed. "I'm really not going to hurt you. You have to believe me."

"I had like a ton to eat today and yesterday," Fredrick offered hesitantly.

"Honey, you're still probably going to die if you leave now." Victoria sighed. "I'm not saying your master was right in killing you, but he was right about one thing, you aren't going to live much longer unless you have food to eat. You probably did eat a lot compared to what you're used to, but you had nowhere near enough to sustain you for long. I'm not allowing you to leave until I can no longer count every single one of your ribs, and that isn't going to be for a while."

"What about the horse hiding in the barn?" Andrew asked looking up at his Father.

"Well, we don't normally have company, and people haven't just popped in since you moved out and married your sister's best friend," Mathew explained.

"It's still not a good idea for them to be in the same spot, especially now that people are likely looking for a brunette runaway in his teens, with a horse, and there's no denying he's a runaway, either from slavery or some prison," Andrew commented. "Although, he's too tanned to be from a prison...."

"I did come from across the border," Fredrick muttered into his knees.

"It's still too close," Andrew objected. "You can't have him here! Anyone can find him, and even if they don't know who his master is, if they discover he's a runaway your likely to be thrown into the second level of prison! You can't do that to them!"

"What about the letter to Philemon from Paul?" Mathew objected. "Slavery's not right Andrew, look at him, even if it is right, it's wrong to treat any living thing like that. His master was going to kill him 'cause he figured he had outlived his usefulness.

He's seventeen, not seventy, the only thing wrong with him is ill treatment."

"I know, I can see that, it's just, what about you?" Andrew sighed.

"What about me? I know God wants me to open up our home to him," Mathew answered. Then as if noticing that he was talking about Fredrick as if he wasn't there he added, "I know God wants us to open our home to you. I want you to feel safe here. God will watch over us under the shadow of his wings, we need not worry about a thing."

"Why do you risk everything for a common slave?" Andrew demanded.

"Two reasons," Mathew finally gave in. "God has a plan for each and every one of us, all we have to do is say yes. Galatians 3:28, 'For there is neither Jew nor Greek, there is neither slave nor free, there is neither male nor female, for you are all one in Christ Jesus.' Do you have that? Jesus loves him, no matter what he's been deemed as by man."

"And the other reason?" Andrew asked, a little softer now.

"He's a malnourished runaway in need of a place to stay, I couldn't not take care of him," Mathew sighed.

"When Matt ran away, it wasn't your fault," Andrew told him.

"He was still my son, and I didn't stop him," Mathew argued.

"We'll find him, he's probably living it up on some street corner, I bet he's fine," Andrew promised. "I'm still worried about you though. There's too much strange activity going on over here. Can't I at least take the horse?"

"Take it," Mathew consented. "If that's what it takes to satisfy you, take it."

"Okay," Andrew nodded. "Ma, Pa, we should probably go back downstairs, Martha, Elizabeth, and their herd of children will probably be back any minute."

"You gonna be okay up here alone?" Mathew asked and Fredrick just nodded. "Alright, if you say so. You're safe here Fredrick." With that he left the room, followed by his oldest son.

"How are you feeling Hun?" Victoria asked walking up to him and resting the back of her hand on his forehead. Fredrick sighed and shrugged.

"My head hurts," He answered honestly.

"Why don't you crawl back in bed if you want, I might have something that will help bring your fever down, and it might help your head too," Victoria told him.

"I didn't know your son ran away, I'm sorry," Fredrick told her sitting on his bed.

"You have nothing to be sorry for," Victoria told him sitting down beside him.

"If I'm making you relive anything..." Fredrick began before Victoria interrupted him.

"Oh Matt ran away about three months ago. You're not making us relive anything that we aren't already living," Victoria answered.

"If it's not too bold to ask, why did Mathew say he didn't stop him?" Fredrick asked.

"It's a long story, for which Mathew blames himself, my youngest son, Johnny, died a couple months before his sixth birthday, it was on his birthday that Matt ran away. They had a fight that morning at breakfast, Matt left the house in a rage and never came back, and Mathew searched nonstop for him until he had to admit that the farm needed his attention. He still searches at night. The man needs to sleep, maybe you'll be good for him, he stayed home all night yesterday, and he hasn't done that in a long time." She explained, then as if trying to convince herself she added: "Besides, Matt's sixteen, I'm sure he can take care of himself, I mean, Martha, Andrew's wife, was younger then that when their first child was born."

"In the past few months you lost two sons?" Fredrick demanded. Sure he had known tragedy in his life, but that was something totally different.

"It's a different kind of grieving for each of them," Victoria told him. "For Johnny it's trying to accept that my little boy is gone and he's not coming back. For Matt, it's trying not to picture him starving or being torn apart by jackals."

"You don't mind that I'm here do you?" Fredrick asked, feeling like his showing up was ripping open wounds in this family that had barely begun to heal.

"I already told you I don't care," She smiled softly, though her eyes were still sad. "Mathew thinks you're exactly what this family needs to learn how to live. I think you've changed my life forever, for the better I hope. Jeremiah 29:11 ''For I know the plans I have for you' declares the Lord, 'plans to welfare you and not for calamity plans to give you a future and a hope." The way I see it, the Lord brought you to us, so it has to work out for the better, even if we can't see it. The Lord doesn't make mistakes."

"I feel like my whole life is a mistake," Fredrick muttered. "Like the only thing I'm good for is doing another man's bidding. I should never have runaway, maybe I am better off dead."

"Now, don't you be saying that, the Lord cares about you so much that he was willing to die for you, he has every hair counted on your head, and he cares about you more than you can imagine," Victoria reprimanded. "Just because sometimes you feel like your good for nothing, doesn't mean it's the truth. In fact, it's just the opposite."

"You and Mathew keep telling me I'm valuable, even your children treat me like I'm their equal, how can I believe any of that when all I've heard my whole life was that I wasn't? I was either the barefoot illiterate child of a man who couldn't afford to feed himself, or I was a thief, a common street rat, a slave, who was more work than he was worth. Someone who was better off dead, because he was to much work to keep alive. I don't even remember what it's like to have a mother, she died giving birth to my sister, who's only a few years younger than me. I'm no one. That's all anyone has ever told me, with the exception of my Father, who was also told he was no one and died when I was twelve."

"I don't think that deep down you believe that," Victoria told him. "You ran away, you must've known somehow that you were worth more than death. The Lord will guide you. He has a plan, and uses everything, good and bad, for his glory, and you're good."

"I've never met anyone with that kind of faith before," Fredrick commented. "Not since my Father died that is. Can love really solve everything? Most people don't even deserve it."

"Now, what would the world come to if we only loved those who loved us?" Victoria chided and Fredrick shrugged, subconsciously playing with his fingers. "I don't know if it solves everything, but I guess if you think about it, if everybody loved everybody, there wouldn't be much wrong in the world would there?"

"That's how it's always been in my life," Fredrick explained. "My sister loved me, and I loved her, everybody else hated me, and the feeling was mutual."

"Everybody else?" Victoria asked softly.

"Unless you count my brother-in-law who ignored my sister, what we had was more like tolerance for each other," Fredrick shrugged. "But it was more then what I had for most people. I guess his daughter wasn't that bad, she was cute, and I liked telling her stories. I don't know if I loved her though, I mean, sure I miss her, but I miss Margret way more." Victoria sighed and gently hugged him.

"Crawl back into bed sweetheart, I'll be back soon with supper and medicine," she announced standing up.

"I'm not really hungry," Fredrick commented.

"I want you to try and eat something," Victoria answered. "Can you do that for me?" Fredrick only nodded.

Slowly, with every gentle word, and every morsel of food she forced into his skinny body, Victoria became the Mother Fredrick never had. She was there for him, from the moment he woke up to the moment he fell asleep. She made him clothes, listened to his problems, and always seemed to know exactly what to say to him when he had a panic attack.

Elizabeth became his best friend, he could talk to her about anything, and she to him. If ever he needed someone to make him laugh, Elizabeth would have him in stitches. Since he wasn't allowed outside he quickly learned household chores, and although she never said, Fredrick could tell she was grateful for the extra help.

As soon as the younger three discovered he loved telling stories, they followed him around all day begging for one. His Father used to make up stories for him and his sister, and Fredrick had inherited his love, and based on the way youngest Couring children couldn't get enough of them, he had also inherited the gift. He told them stories his Father had told him, and almost every one that he had made up for Liesel or Margret, not to mention countless stories that he made up just for them.

As slowly as he accepted Victoria and the children though, Mathew was even slower. Slowly, once Fredrick became convinced that Mathew wasn't going to beat him for a mistake or not working hard enough, he almost subconsciously tried to see if Mathew would beat him, or kick him out of his house, for being a brat, but Mathew never so much as raised his voice.

Finally, Mathew's unending kindness, patience, and hospitality, convinced Fredrick of something he hadn't expected. Mathew loved him. Whether it was waking up screaming in the middle of the night, or cowering from the man who wouldn't hurt a fly, or later on, completely ignoring him, Mathew never seemed to get mad at him. Fredrick had lived at the Courings house for almost two months when it finally hit him, that Mathew's freedom was in danger, and Mathew didn't care, as long as Fredrick's could be secure.

Eventually, Fredrick's arms grew meat on them, and then muscle, not much obviously since he almost never went outside, but enough.

When the day came that Victoria could no longer count every single one of his ribs, Fredrick surprised himself by not wanting to leave.

***

"You've already heard all my stories," Fredrick sighed one evening as Laura begged him for one. He was fairly content to just sit on the ground and stare into the warm fire.

"Well then retell one," Ethel added.

"Or make another one up," Aaron added.

"It's actually not that easy to just make up a story at the drop of a hat," Fredrick told him.

"Well then retell one," Aaron begged.

"Yeah, your stories never get old!" Laura smiled leaning on his knee.

"Never huh?" Fredrick sighed again. He knew, as well as Aaron, Ethel and Laura did that if they begged for one long enough he was bound to tell them a story, for one thing he loved telling stories, and another, he felt like they deserved to just be kids every once in a while.

Mathew, Victoria and Elizabeth sat around in chairs, every evening was the same in this house. Victoria or Elizabeth would light a fire in the fireplace, and the whole family would gather in the sitting room as the rest of the house froze until either Mathew or Victoria decided it was time for the younger three to go to bed. More often than not Fredrick ended up telling a story, he was secretly convinced that just because the kids were the only ones asking, Elizabeth and their parents loved to hear his stories just as much.

"How about a true story?" He finally decided. Instantly he had everyone's full attention, it was the first time he had ever offered a true story, and everyone was seemingly intrigued.

"Yes," Elizabeth agreed enthusiastically when everyone else was silent, and Laura snuggled herself under one of his arms.

"Okay, I was about five or six I think…" he began and instantly began reliving the tale.

*"Thunder cracked and I leaped to my feet wide eyed and terrified. My father glanced up at from the various bowls and pots catching the worst of the water leaking through the roof.*

*"My Father had the same colour of hair and eyes as I did, but his eyes were different. They saw all the good things in the world, they loved even the lowest and the worst people alive. They always seemed to have a glow of happiness in them. When his arms were wrapped around you, you felt like the safest person alive.*

*"Can't sleep?" He sighed looking over at me.*

*"It's loud," I complained. Lightning flashed again, followed by another clap of thunder, and beside me Margret whimpered on the floor mat.*

*"Alright, come here guys." He sighed, clearly deciding that despite his efforts the storm was just too severe to sleep. We each climbed onto one of his laps, resting our tired heads on his shoulders, and he wrapped his arms around us. 'You aren't afraid of a little thunder are you? God has complete control over the storm. Don't you remember the story of how Jesus told the storm to be quiet?"*

*"Yeah, Jesus was sleeping in the back of a boat, so the disciples woke him up, and he told the storm to be quiet, and it was!" Margret answered. Just as she finished saying that there was another flash of lightning, and clap of thunder, causing both of us to jump.*

*"Why can't Jesus tell this storm to be quiet?" I complained and Father laughed. His deep laugh, which came straight from his belly, and lit up his whole face.*

*"It's good for the soil Fredrick," Father told me. "Besides, that's not the only story of thunder in the bible, sometimes the thunder cracked because God himself was talking. Like when he was talking to Moses on the top of a mountain, all the Hebrews could hear on the bottom of the hill was thunder cracking." The room lit up again and Father gently rubbed our arms.*

*"Well, why does God have to talk so loud?"* Margret complained, *just as the thunder cracked.*

*"Well, sometimes if he talked quietly, nobody would listen. Everybody's tried to ignore him, some spend their whole lives trying to ignore him, he's hoping to get your attention,"* Father answered. *"Are you ready to listen?"*

"Then what happened?" Mathew asked when Fredrick stopped talking.

"I don't really remember," Fredrick shrugged, half aware that Laura was falling asleep on his shoulder. "We probably waited till the storm was over, then fell asleep in his bed like we always did when we were that age. I do know that I wasn't ready to listen then but... I think I am now."

"Then answer him," Mathew told him gently.

"I don't know how, I've spent so long ignoring him, I don't really know how to answer him," Fredrick answered.

"Well, then just tell him your sorry for ignoring him, that you're done ignoring him, and you want to live your life for him from now on," Mathew answered.

"Okay," Fredrick answered slowly, then, in front of everyone, he accepted Christ.

# CHAPTER 6

Matt Couring sank against the cold wall in exhaustion. There was almost no light down there, but he didn't need light to hear the soft moans, or the chains rattling against the wall. He didn't need light to hear the cries of someone being whipped a ways away. He didn't need light to smell the stench of vomit and unwashed bodies.

"Matt!" the head prison guard yelled. Matt leaped to his feet and glanced over at him, silently hoping that he wasn't in trouble... again....

***

Andrew grabbed a bucket and began milking the camel that had been a wedding gift from his Father. He hadn't been to his Father's house in months, and Pa hadn't been here. He saw his family at church, but that was it. He wouldn't admit it, but was worried about them, almost as much as he was worried about Matt. Then there was that horse.

Andrew finished milking the cow and gently petted Blackjack. He had no idea what the horse's real name was, or the name of the runaway, so he had ended up just calling the horse Blackjack.

"I sure hope you don't end up being more trouble than your worth." He sighed. He grabbed a brush and ran it down Blackjack's coat, then plopped some wheat down for Blackjack and the camel to share, laid some grain down for the chickens to eat, picked up the milk pail, and wondered into the house.

"Papa!" Mary-Liz (short for Mary-Elizabeth after her Aunt) exclaimed once he came in. Andrew set the bucket by the doorpost, just as his daughter ran into his welcoming arms.

"Hey Princess, did you have a good day?" He asked swinging her above his head before sitting her on one of his arms.

"Yep!" She grinned. "I made supper!"

"You did?" Andrew smiled.

"Uh-huh." She smiled, her blonde hair that fell in curls to her shoulders and looked so much like her Mother's, bounced up and down as she vigorously nodded her head.

"She made circles with my wooden spoon, in a pot, on the floor, for an hour." Martha smiled softly looking at him from over the hearth.

"Sounds like she made supper to me," Andrew answered returning her soft smile, then lowering his two year old to the floor. "Alright, go play Mary."

"Are you okay Drew?" Martha asked gently as Mary-Liz ran off.

"I'm fine," Andrew answered washing the dirt off of his hands and collapsing at the table, which was like the only furniture in the house save for a cradle, trundle bed, and the big bed.

"You've been saying that for months now, you won't let me or the kids go over to your parents' house, you never laugh anymore, and you're always tired," Martha answered.

"I'm just not sleeping very well," he answered plainly. "And you don't want to burn supper, you should take care of that."

"Our supper's fine," Martha answered sitting across the table from him. "You're not. Why won't you talk to me?"

"Just trust me okay? It's for your own safety," Andrew answered.

"Drew, are you okay?" Martha demanded. Andrew hesitated, it had been nine months and nothing had happened, other than his marriage getting more and more strained.

"My parents have an escaped slave in their house alright?" Andrew finally let out.

"What?" Martha demanded, then jumped to her feet. "That's what you haven't been telling me?"

"I didn't want you to know, you were safer not knowing," Andrew told her slouching in his chair.

"I'm fine, the slave's not even in this house," Martha sighed.

"His horse is in the barn though..." Andrew sighed.

"Drew, you know you can tell me anything right?" Martha asked.

"I know I can, but your safety is worth more than anything to me," Andrew answered standing up.

"How do you know about all of this?" She demanded.

"I saw him, the slave, it was the day after he showed up," Andrew answered leaning against the table, staring into space. "I had never seen anyone that skinny before, Martha he was half dead! He looked like he was going to pass out, and his back had so many lashes on it." Martha sighed, got up from around the table, and then sat down on his lap.

"God has everything under control, remember?" Martha reminded him.

"I can't get his face out of my mind, there was nothing to him but skin and bones. His eyes, they were hollow, if my parents hadn't taken him in he would've died out there. Everything about him said hunger or abuse. I called him a common slave and told my parents to feed him and send him on his way. I didn't even know I could be that heartless."

"You were scared," Martha told him.

"My mother's gone through enough, she can't lose my father, and if she loses that boy..." Andrew began then stopped, unable to form the thoughts out loud. "I love you, and I'm sorry I banned you from visiting your best friend, but I can't let you go over there with the kids," Andrew whispered as his wife almost fell into his arms.

"I know, it's okay, I see her every Sunday at Church anyway," Martha whispered. "And remember, 'which of you by worrying can add a single hour to his span of life?' Everything is going to be okay honey."

She sat on his lap for a while longer until Jonathan got hungry, and Mary-Liz decided she wanted Andrew to play babies with her. About five minutes later supper was burnt, again.

\*\*\*

"With only a short distance left till they reached home, they were suddenly swept into a sandstorm, unlike anything they had ever seen before. Elaine reached for her sister's hand, terrified to lose her again, and pulled her to the ground. Protecting her from the powerful winds and sands with her own arms. Before they knew it, they were buried in the earth. They say they're still lost, somewhere just under the surface of the desert," Fredrick explained dramatically from his bed. Ethel and Laura sat at the foot of the bed, and Aaron lay sprawled out on his own bed. Elizabeth, who had brought her sewing upstairs and was sitting on the trunk, suddenly put it down and stared at him.

"They just died? But Elaine spent forever looking for her lost sister to bring her home, and they're never even gonna get to go home?" Elizabeth demanded.

"Everyone's gotta die sometime," Fredrick grinned. "It's adventurous, with kidnappers and stowaways, but yeah, I guess it is kind of a sad story. I made it up this morning before I woke Aaron up."

"You make up a lot of stories when you're trying to get Aaron up," Ethel commented.

"It's the best time to think," Fredrick grinned, he didn't say what he was thinking that stories were his way of hiding from the world when it ran out of his control. Even if his stories were sad, or scary, they were small things at least he could control.

"Can you tell us another story?" Laura asked.

"Someone else has to talk now, I just told an hour long story, my voice needs to rest," Fredrick told her.

"That's fair." Elizabeth nodded. "And I have to go make supper, so see you later."

They made small talk for a while until supper was ready, and after prayers were said, then Mathew began to speak.

"Harvest is ready to be brought in," he explained, as the six casually glanced at him. It wasn't news to any of them. "Everyone knows that I haven't had any less than two sons help bring in the harvest in about a decade, Matt would be nineteen now right? Anyway, quite frankly, I'm not as young as I was ten years ago, I think it wouldn't be to suspicious if I hired a seventeen year old to help bring in the harvest."

"You want Fredrick to go outside?" Elizabeth demanded.

"Well, since he's shown up here he's gotten stronger, taller, and you actually can't see any of the scars in his back unless you look closely, and I don't see why anyone would. Andrew's been taking Lightning to town for a while now and nobody's confronted him yet, and nobody seems to suspect us of anything strange. We've have a perfect opportunity to do so. If we don't do it now, we won't have another excuse to let him outside till spring, hiring a seventeen year old for the harvest is perfect," Mathew explained. "Plus, we could really use the help."

"I'm eighteen," Fredrick pointed out. "And that sounds pretty nice."

"Since when are you eighteen?" Aaron asked. "You said you were seventeen."

"First of all, that was nine months ago, second, I turned eighteen last month," Fredrick shrugged.

"Your birthday was a month ago and you didn't even say anything!?" Elizabeth demanded.

"I didn't think it was that big of a deal," Fredrick shrugged.

"It's a huge deal," Elizabeth argued.

"You could have at least told us," Mathew told him, looking slightly amused.

"I honestly didn't even realize my birthday had passed until like a week later, and I think I had a brief moment of 'hey, I'm eighteen now' and it was over." Fredrick shrugged.

"You're hopeless," Elizabeth complained.

The next day, when Fredrick went outside, the sunshine on his face was probably the most beautiful thing he had ever felt, he had no idea how much he missed it. Even the dust blowing around him, so hard it beat against his face, felt wonderful. Then, Elizabeth surprised him with a birthday cake at supper. Apparently, his birthday was a big deal, and they were going to celebrate it, even if it was a month late.

# CHAPTER 7

"Am I gonna have to go back into hiding come winter?" Fredrick asked just after falling into bed a few weeks later.

"How am I gonna know that?" Aaron asked, rolling over in his bed. "I do know that I miss your stories!"

"Just wait till I'm not exhausted every day, then I'll tell you stories till your heart's content," Fredrick smiled, although he rolled his eyes as he did it. "And I still tell stories on Sundays."

"That's true." Aaron shrugged. After a pause he added, "Fredrick, do you still think about your sister all the time?"

"Yeah," he muttered softly. "I think about when we were children, about when we were little kids without a care in the world, I think about now, I can't help but wonder if she's even alive. She's in every dream, every time I can't distract my thoughts, she fills them. Why?"

"Cause, I can fill my days with distractions, but every night, I miss my brothers." Aaron sighed.

"I know it's hard, I wish I could make it better for you but I can't." Fredrick sighed.

"It's gotten to the point where I think I'm used to three or four hours of sleep every night. Matt left us, like there was something wrong with us or something, why? What's so wrong with me that he didn't want to be my brother anymore?" Aaron demanded and Fredrick sighed, at a loss for what to say. As far as he knew Aaron hadn't even talked about either of his brothers being gone ever, and he chose Fredrick to open up to? Fredrick, who was so caught up in his own anger and fear that he could barely control himself?

"Nothing is wrong with you," Fredrick finally said. "And Matt is stupid if he couldn't realize what a great kid you are. Matt ran away from his problems, he can't face them, and he's still running. My guess is that he's scared to face them. It has everything to do with Matt, and nothing to do with you."

"Do you think there's birthday cake in heaven?" Aaron asked. Apparently they were discussing both brothers tonight... great, now Fredrick was going to be so depressed he wasn't going to sleep either

"Um..." Fredrick muttered unsure what the correct answer was. "I don't think they have time there, but I dunno, there's probably cake..."

"Do you think Matt's okay?" Aaron sighed.

"Maybe," Fredrick answered, silently praying Aaron would stop asking him questions he didn't know the answer too, especially about his brothers... "Why?"

"Tomorrow would be Johnny's eighth birthday, and it's also the one year anniversary of Matt running away," Aaron answered.

"I see," Fredrick nodded. "I bet angels make good birthday cake."

"Do you like Elizabeth?" Aaron asked randomly, and Fredrick almost choked.

"How old are you?" Fredrick demanded. "I'm not getting into this with a 12 year old!"

"I'm going to be thirteen in two months, do you like my sister or not?"

"It's complicated," Fredrick muttered.

"How?" Aaron demanded.

"Well, if you promise not to tell anyone, she is really cute, and she's got a great personality. Not to mention a really admirable faith, but if you tell anyone I said that, I swear you will be so dead!" Fredrick answered.

"Two things, first of all: I knew you liked her! I think she likes you too. You guys would actually make a cute couple, and if it comes to it, I'd approve of you as a brother-in-law," Aaron exclaimed.

"I said I liked her, not 'I love her and want to spend the rest of my like with her!'" Fredrick groaned. "Besides, it doesn't really work that way, you seriously can't tell anyone, especially Lizzie, I said that okay?"

"Yeah don't worry about it, your secret's safe with me. Anyway, second of all: You threatened me... You've never done that before."

"Sorry..." Fredrick replied unsure where he was going with that.

"Do you know what this means?" Aaron asked excitedly. "No one has ever threatened me except for Andrew or Matt, so that means that you think of me as a little brother!"

"Oh," Fredrick answered, unsure about Aaron's logic. Frankly he was just wondering where that came from, he must've picked it up from the Courings, because he couldn't remember ever playfully threatening anybody...

"So, do you?" Aaron asked.

"Do I what?" Fredrick yawned.

"Do you think of me as a little brother?"

"Yeah, I do," he told him without hesitation. "You're a pretty awesome kid."

"Cool." Aaron yawned, and in just a few minutes Fredrick heard the sound of his breathing change and was shocked to realize he was asleep, half convinced he had never fallen asleep that fast in his life. Fredrick sighed, as tired as he was he stared up at the roof and whispered a prayer.

"God, thank you for bringing me here, honestly I haven't felt this much at peace since before my father died and through this family I came to know you. But Lord, please be with Margret, I hate to think of her, still enslaved and I don't even know if she's still alive. Please Lord, if she is alive still, don't let her die without you. Also, apparently tomorrow is Johnny's would be birthday, and the one year anniversary of Matt's disappearance. Please be with the Courings tomorrow, and Lord, if it's not too much to ask, please let Matt be okay, and could he come home safely?" Finishing off his prayer he closed his eyes and fell fast asleep, and didn't wake up again until the sunlight hit him in the face.

"Good morning," Fredrick chirped sitting up. Across the room Aaron groaned and pulled the covers over his head. "You're almost more amusing in the mornings then you are annoying, and that's saying something. Rise and shine farm boy, you've got cows to milk, horses to groom, although don't fret over it too much, it's Sunday so we aren't going out into the fields, but you are getting out of bed. It is a beautiful day, out there."

"Why are you always so giddy and cheerful in the morning?" Aaron growled through the covers.

"Why are you always so grouchy and lazy in the morning? And talkative at night?" Fredrick replied tossing him some clothes and quickly getting dressed himself. "Breakfast will be served for those who work for it, if half the barn is still a mess you will miss it, as is the usual."

Aaron groaned, rolled over and groaned again. He lay so still Fredrick was about 90% certain he had fallen back asleep. He sighed and got dressed before grabbing Aaron's shoulder and shaking it.

"Why does morning always have to come so early?" Aaron snarled.

Fredrick rolled his eyes, deciding that a question that stupid didn't deserve to be justified with an answer. Feeling generous he did Aaron's chores for him before going upstairs to continue to fight with him. Since that day was Sunday, family went to church while Fredrick wondered around the house bored, then they came home for lunch. It was just after, the little girls were still doing dishes, when Elizabeth came in and squatted in front of him.

"What are you thinking?" She asked staring at his face. Fredrick met her gaze and shrugged.

"Nothing."

"Your always thinking nothing, I think 90% of the time a more accurate response would be 'nothing I care to go into detail about.'"

"That's just 'cause you know me to well, most people that would just get more questions if I answered that."

"Probably," Elizabeth shrugged. She stood and pulled Fredrick to his feet by his wrist. "C'mon, I wanna show you something, now that you're allowed outside."

"Okay," Fredrick answered warily, Elizabeth led him out of the house, and Fredrick didn't complain when she didn't let go of his wrist until after they left the house. Fredrick followed Elizabeth about half a step behind her till they got to a little oasis a little ways away from the Courings farm. "So this is the oasis I keep hearing about."

"Andrew and Matt used to take me out here when we were kids. Then they out grew it and I used to take my little brothers and sisters out here," Elizabeth explained. "I like coming out here alone though, It's a good place to think."

"Yeah, it's nice," Fredrick agreed sitting beside it and dipping his hands in the water. He sensed she wanted to talk, but either way he took his shoes and socks off and dipped his feet in the water. "My father used to take my sister and I out to an oasis like this all the time and we'd build sand castles and wade in the creek while our Father watched on the edge. Sometimes he'd join us, and he used to play games with us, somehow playing with Father made using imagination so much better," Fredrick answered. He paused and waited to see if Elizabeth would reply, but she wordlessly sat down on the rocks and rested her feet in the water. Fredrick sighed and sat next to her. "What's up?"

"Today would've been Johnny's seventh birthday, and it's also the one year anniversary of Matt's disappearance," Elizabeth answered.

"Yeah, Aaron told me that last night, keep going, I'm here to listen," Fredrick told her.

"We figured he had just gone away to think or something," Elizabeth explained. "Pa told Aaron and Matt to hurry up so they could get as much work done today as possible. For some reason after Johnny died Ma withdrew herself from her work, and Pa threw himself into his work. Matt responded more like Ma did, and unfortunately Pa wouldn't accept that. Matt groaned and looked at him, he said that the work would still be there tomorrow. They got into this huge fight, finally Matt shoved his chair away from the table and ran out of the house, slamming the door so hard the house shook. Pa got up and started to follow him, telling him to get back in the house, but Ma stopped him and told him to let him grieve his own way.

When breakfast was over Pa and Aaron went to the fields, Ma went to her room, me and the girls did the house work. The girls and I assumed he must've gone to the oasis or something, I mean, where else would he be? Even when Ethel went to get water for lunch and reported he wasn't there, nobody thought anything of it. Maybe he had gone to the fields after all, or he was gone on a walk. Lunch came and went, Pa said he'd show up when he was hungry, but Ma was stressed out cause she said it wasn't like him to miss a meal, which it wasn't. Honestly, Matt was still in that stage where boys see food and they just inhale it. I was starting to worry too, but whatever right? Maybe Pa was right, he'd show up when he was hungry.

"When supper time came and Matt still wasn't back, Even Pa started to get nervous. He wouldn't admit to it though, but I could tell. He told us all to stay at home, and said he was going to go look for Matt. He came back at about 8:00 to see if Matt had returned when he was out looking. He left shortly after that, and got Andrew to help him look. Me, Ma, and Aaron wanted to go help, but he told Ma and I that we had to take care of the children, although I think he meant I needed to take care of Ma, and he told Aaron he was too young to wander about the streets at night."

"Laura fell asleep on the floor and I carried her up to bed, although I sent Ethel up when she was still falling asleep. Ma kept crying about how now she lost two of her sons now till she finally cried herself to sleep in the sitting room. I wanted to send Aaron up to his bed, but he had a complete meltdown and said he didn't want to go to bed alone. It wasn't until that moment that I realized, he hadn't slept in a room by himself before. I made him some tea but he couldn't even finish it he was so tired, I let him sleep in my bed. I fell asleep in Matt's bed, which is now your bed. I'm half convinced Aaron still hasn't slept alone in a room before. If he hasn't told you this, then don't tell him you know, but after Matt ran away he used to come into our room and sleep on the floor. Other times he would sleep on the floor of Ma and Pa's room."

"I learned the next morning Andrew had sent Pa home to bed at two in the morning, claiming it would be easier to look when there was light out. It was kind of ironic that we were the last ones to go to bed, and the first ones up, but we were both up with the first light of dawn. I made him eat something, then he left to go look for Matt. Nearly all the men we knew helped search for him, we notified the police, and a bunch of women came over and cried with Ma. The searchers gave up after a week, Andrew said it was a hopeless search after two weeks, and Pa...he was devastated."

"God never promised life would be easy," Fredrick answered, unsure exactly how he was supposed to reply.

"How could Matt do that? It totally crushed our parents, who were still grieving over the death of Johnny, I thought for sure they'd break. I wish I knew he was okay, but I'm so angry with him, I don't know. The police don't even care, or else they would've found him by now wouldn't they?" Elizabeth asked. Fredrick was at a total loss of how to reply to that, and made no reply other than wrapping his arm around her shoulders. To his surprise she rested her head on his chest and broke down into tears.

"I hate him." She sobbed. "There, I said it and I don't care, I hate him. He did probably the most selfish thing he could have possibly done, and didn't even care.

"Things were a mess before you showed up, honestly when Ma made you those clothes it was the first time I had seen her work for that long without stopping. I just started making all the meals after

Johnny died because she would forget what she was doing and burn the food. I was doing a ton of half-finished chores, cause she would leave the floor half swept, or she would leave the dishes still in the tub, or half the furniture would be dusted, or half the clothes would be hanging on the line, the other half were still wet in the bucket. I practically had to follow her around all day picking up after her. I had three little siblings who still needed a mother, and she couldn't do that so I had too. Especially the girls, I had to make sure they did their homework, and their chores, and they still got the attention and love they needed.

"Pa was no help, after Johnny died he got so strict. He didn't really talk to anyone unless he was telling them what to do. After Matt left, it got even worse. Ma would spend so much time in her room I couldn't help but wonder what she was doing up there, Pa walked around in a daze. All I wanted was for my parents to be normal again. I don't know, I guess it's kind of selfish to think like that."

"You're allowed to grieve you know," Fredrick told her. "Things were bound to change of course, but you are allowed to be upset."

"Why would he run away?" Elizabeth demanded.

"Is that and actual question, or something your just throwing out there?" Fredrick quizzed.

"Why do people runaway?" Elizabeth asked. The tone of her voice said that the first one was probably a statement, but now she realized she was talking to someone who had runaway as well. For totally different reasons, with a totally different story obviously, but still, a runaway none the less.

"They're afraid live, but they can't die cause they're afraid to die. They want a better life, and even if they have everything they could ever want, like in the case of Matt, he was probably so depressed, and so caught up in his grief he thought he had nothing but the hope that maybe things will be better somewhere else." Fredrick sighed.

"You gave my parents reason to live," Elizabeth told him raising her head to look at him, her tears starting to dwindle.

"What do you mean?"

"I don't know, it's like you showed up and my parents realized that they were still needed. I don't know if you know this, but when you showed up, you were half dead, you were skin and bones, wearing nothing but oversized rags, and your back was covered in lashes. You aren't like that anymore thankfully, but every time anyone told you to do something you got scared of them. You obeyed as quickly as possible, with this look on your face like 'please don't hurt me!' My Father had to change, I think he was scared you were going to have a mental breakdown. As for my mother, I don't really know. She still leaves her chores half finished, and I'm not really brave enough to let her cook, but Aaron, Ethel, and Laura have a mother again."

"I guess it's possible..." Fredrick muttered.

"It is," Elizabeth told him. "I watched it happen. Of course, that brings on new worries. If you're caught, my Father would be arrested, and I don't think my Mother can handle you both leaving in chains. I don't think I can handle it. Even if it was just one of you I couldn't handle it."

"The Lord keeps us in the palm of his hand Elizabeth," Fredrick reminded her.

"You know for someone who is a new Christian, or even someone who's been a Christian their whole lives, you have amazing faith." She sighed.

# CHAPTER 8

"What would I do if you were caught though?" Elizabeth sighed pulling away from Fredrick's arms.

"I don't know, don't fret about it okay?" Fredrick told her. Elizabeth sighed making gentle waves in the water with her hand. For a while the two of them sat in comfortable silence before Elizabeth piped up again.

"What does it feel like?"

"What does what feel like?" Fredrick demanded.

"To be a prisoner," Elizabeth answered simply. "Or to be free, and know your sister is still a prisoner."

"Okay, you are not taking my advice not to fret about it are you?" Fredrick sighed. He studied her for a few minutes then shrugged. "As for knowing my sister is still a prisoner, I don't know, it's hard to say. Probably no different than it feels to not know if Matt's okay."

"But how did you become a slave? I mean, I know you stole, but I don't know, you're so good at telling stories, but the only true story you've ever told me, or anyone as far as I know, is the story about how the thunder scared you and your sister. Which was an awesome story by the way, and it was really cool you became a Christian, but what about the rest of your childhood? Can't you tell me about that?"

"That's a really heavy story," Fredrick commented.

"It's a heavy day," Elizabeth argued.

"Exactly, why do you want more on your chest?" Fredrick asked.

"Cause I wanna know," Elizabeth answered.

"Alright, how about we make a deal, I'll tell you about the deepest parts of my life, if you tell me about Johnny and Matt?" Fredrick bargained.

"I already told you about the day Matt ran away," Elizabeth answered. "And I'm not as good at telling stories as you, but I guess I can. Johnny was a healthy baby, but when he was about three or four he started to get sick, if ever he ran too much, or he was surrounded by too much dust, he used to start coughing and wheezing. All of us we so protective of him because of that. Ma and Pa never let him wander to far from the house, so we used to make up calmer games to play with him in the house.

"As much as we all adored him, he was closest with Matt. Watching the two of them was so beautiful. Johnny couldn't run around obviously, so Matt used to hike him onto his back and run for him. The two of them would laugh for hours. It wasn't uncommon for Matt and Johnny to spend an entire summer's day together. When Matt was all but collapsed on the ground from exhaustion Johnny would still be laughing and begging for more. Sometimes you would find Matt, totally exhausted with sweat completely covering his body, laying on his back with Johnny sitting on his stomach, his adorable smile was always there, and so big.

"That kid was such a spoiled little brat, he had six big siblings and a sister in law wrapped around his little finger, and two parents who doubted he'd even live as long as he did. That kid knew how to get what he wanted, when he wanted. Like for example, even though he was sick, he decided he wanted to move out of the trundle bed and into the 'big boy's room.' Ma and Pa weren't sure it was a good idea, 'cause he'd wake up a lot in the middle of the night unable to breath and of course, one of them would have to wake up with him. But he eventually got Matt on board with him, and he promised to take care of Johnny if he got an attack in the middle of the night. It was only a couple months before he moved out of Ma and Pa's room and into the room you're in now. At first he shared a bed with

Aaron. It was only a couple weeks though before he moved from Aaron's bed to Matt's bed.

"Matt kept his word, whenever Johnny got sick in the middle of the night Matt would get up with him. I don't know what he would do exactly when he had a breathing attack in the middle of the night, but I do know even though both Ma and Pa told Matt he could wake them up, he didn't usually. If Johnny was really bad or something, Matt would have naps in the middle of the day. Ma took care of Johnny during the day, Matt got the night shift, and Pa got early mornings, meal times, and evenings, so all together they each got about a third of the day. Me and Aaron would take care of the work that they neglected.

There were times when I would wake up in the middle of the night for a glass of water and Matt would be sitting in the armchair just holding Johnny as he gasped in his arms. There were probably countless nights where Matt would just hold Johnny till he fell asleep, sometimes even longer. There were so many times when I would wake up to make breakfast and Matt would be holding Johnny, telling him a bible story or something. Johnny wouldn't even look like he was listening, he just looked tired, but breathing was so hard he couldn't sleep.

"Matt was so patient, gentle, caring, but when Johnny died, something inside of him died as well. He and Ma reacted the same way, they just stopped living. There were times when they would be doing something, simple, like getting a glass of water, and they'd just start staring into space. Neither of them could focus on anything. Pa was the opposite, he focused on nothing but what he was doing at that time. I guess I was more like that, but I was mostly concerned with Aaron, Ethel and Laura still having a mother. Pa was usually really patient with Ma and Matt. He knew they were grieving in their own way that was different then his way of grieving, but on Johnny's would-be birthday of all days, he snapped. That's when Matt ran away."

"Yeah, see, you're not that bad at telling stories," Fredrick told her.

"Are you crying?" Elizabeth demanded.

"Lump in my throat, there's a difference," Fredrick argued.

Elizabeth half smiled and rolled her eyes. "Your turn."

"Okay..." Fredrick began ordering the lump to go away. "My Mother died giving birth to my sister when I was two, so I don't remember her at all. It was always just Father, Margret and me. It was all I knew, and I loved it. Father would tell us stories about our Mother, stories from the bible, and stories that he's make up. He couldn't read, but he had learned a lot of the stories at church and he retold a lot of them to us. He would send us to get our nightclothes on, then we would return, sit on his lap, and he'd tell us a story by the fireplace.

"When I was about eight, my father was robbed. Literally. A drunk came into the house with a knife and held it to Margret's throat until my Father gave up everything he owned. When the drunk left we had furniture and a house, basically the only things the drunk couldn't carry, but my Father just held my sister and the two of them cried in each other's arms for a long time. Eventually he called me over, and he just held us, he didn't let us go for a long time.

"We eventually found out the drunk was actually hired by a rich man, I don't know why he chose a working class widower with two young children to pick on, it wasn't like we had much to begin with, but shortly after that he told my father's boss that he wasn't an honest worker. It wasn't true of course, but my Father was fired either way.

"We sold what little we had left, and moved into a leaky one room apartment. Father had no money, he started working odd jobs, begging even. He usually scraped together enough money to pay the rent, sometimes late, and the landlord would threaten to kick us out, but he always got enough. Margret and I got one small meal every day, Father rarely joined us though. We were little kids, we didn't realize he was starving himself so we could eat. I don't think we even gave it a second thought. My Father died when I was ten, so Margret and I moved again, this time to the streets.

"We survived by working odd jobs, begging, and stealing. We had no other way of surviving. I found out who the rich man was that took everything from us. Our Father had been careful to hide it from us, but I found out. I left Margret in the alleyway, and planned to meet her there in the evening, then I sneaked into his house, planning to steal from him. It wasn't anything compared to what he took from us but I had to do it. I probably could have done it without getting caught, but I don't know. Maybe I wanted to get caught, so I could look into the eyes of the man who stole everything from us. So I could see if his eyes really did have nothing but cold blooded cruelty in them.

"A street rat stealing from your kitchen really isn't that big of a crime. It's a crime, but it's too petty to warrant the death sentence. Public flogging is usually the punishment, I've actually had that a couple times, other times the punishment is selling the beggar to pay the debt. Jason saw me, he knew that I knew, and that somehow he had to shut me up, since I was a repeat offender, it was easy, he just asked that I become his slave. Margret found me about a week later, and against my warnings, sold herself into slavery so she could be with me, and get food."

"That's really sad," Elizabeth sighed.

"Yeah, I guess so, no more than your story, it's just different." Fredrick shrugged. "I wish Margret was here though, she's paying for my crimes while I'm safe and free, but she's fiercely loyal. She wouldn't leave her husband and stepdaughter."

"I wouldn't really describe you as 'safe' but I can see where you're coming from," Elizabeth agreed. "That would be hard."

"So what do you think? Now that you know I'm a thief? Your parents know, but we never talk about it. It's like it doesn't even register to them. What do you think though?" Fredrick asked.

"I don't know, where else were you going to get food? Besides, if there was someone I could blame for Johnny's death you can be pretty sure I'd try to extract revenge myself. Jason hadn't even stolen your freedom, or your sister's freedom yet, and he had already taken more than just your father's life. I don't know if I would do the exact same things you did, but I really don't blame you for it. Besides, my Pa used to say 'you can't judge someone for doing something before they knew Christ. If they don't know Christ and they're steeped in sin, don't worry about it, and just love them. If they claim to know Christ and they're still steeped in sin, well then don't tell everyone else, tell them when the two of you are alone," Elizabeth answered. "In other words, so what if you stole some stuff? You were hungry, and the other time, by human standards, you were pretty justified in doing so. You weren't a Christian back then, and you don't steal anymore anyway. Why would I care?"

"Because you're perfect," Fredrick muttered.

"Oh, I'm far from perfect. The difference is people have made some sins worse than other sins, but in the bible, murder and jealousy are on the same list, Murder isn't even on the top, it's like sixth on the list," Elizabeth told him.

"Was that another quote from your Father?" Fredrick asked.

"No, that was mine!" Elizabeth responded, faking offence.

"Well, it just sounded really wise so I was wondering," Fredrick explained raising his hands in defence. Elizabeth answered that by punching his arm.

# CHAPTER 9

It had been ten months since Fredrick first showed up, and thirteen months since Matt had runaway. Elizabeth punched a large pile of dough with the palm of her hand and glanced over at her sisters at the other end of the table. Ethel mending a pair of Aaron's trousers, and Laura rocking her rag doll. Ma was asleep, Pa, Aaron and Fredrick out in the fields. The house was quiet like it usually was in the middle of the day. No one talked, each did their own thing.

"*Lord, I feel helpless,*" She prayed in her head, beating bread dough. "*Frightened even. I miss my brothers. All three of them. I'm worried about Fredrick, in more ways than one. I'm sick of this limbo phrase, waiting to be caught, waiting to be freed. Waiting for news of Matt's death, waiting for him to come home. Waiting for Andrew to feel safe here again, waiting for it to feel normal that he's scared of his childhood home.*"

Just then there was a knock on the door, and Elizabeth, lost in her own thoughts, jumped. She wiped her hands on her apron and slipped another apron on to hide the flour covering the apron underneath before opened the door, wondering who showed up for company these days anyway.

"Martha!" she exclaimed, her eyes wide in shock and delight. "What are you doing here? Where are the kids? Did you walk this whole way? Didn't Andrew say it wasn't a good idea for you to come over here? Why are you here?"

"Hold on Eliz, one question at a time please! Can I come in?" Martha answered, though she didn't smile, and seemed awfully serious. Elizabeth stepped out of the way for her friend and sister in law to walk into the house.

"Would you like me to take your shawl?" Elizabeth asked.

"No, I'm not staying long, your brother is home alone with two toddlers and need to be back before his sanity is gone. This was urgent though, where's the runaway?"

"What runaway?"

"You don't have to play dumb with me, Andrew told me the whole story, where is he?"

"In the fields with Pa and Aaron, why?"

"Hey girls, why don't you go upstairs and play?" Martha asked.

"But I'm busy," Ethel argued.

"Ethel, take Laura and the trousers upstairs, and don't argue," Elizabeth lectured. Ethel sighed, scooped the trousers up, and grabbed Laura's hand, obviously bitter about be treated like one of the 'little girls'.

"Andrew ran into trouble in town today, that horse the runaway stole, whatever his original name was, we call him Blackjack, anyway, some guy showed up and said that Blackjack was stolen. Andrew was able to convince him that he had taken the horse in an honest deal, but he's still high on the suspicion list, and the man has the horse, he's looking for the thief," Martha rushed through her words.

"Okay, that is pretty urgent... um, alright... do you know what the man's name was?" Elizabeth answered, wrapping her shawl around her arms.

"I don't know, I wasn't there, Jason something or another?"

\*\*\*

Fredrick glanced up to see Elizabeth, and another girl run towards him. The other girl stopped when she was a few feet away from him, though Elizabeth ran straight into his arms and clung to his torso. She started talking so fast the only thing he caught was something about her brother and hiding.

"Hold on, Elizabeth breath, and enunciate your words," Fredrick ordered pushing her back so he could look at her face.

"Fredrick, Jason Cummings is here," Elizabeth gasped, and suddenly the air got really thick and hard to breathe.

"Are you sure?" Fredrick demanded, trying to sound not totally terrified, but his voice shook, even in his own head.

"Mostly, apparently a man took Lighting while Andrew was in town, claiming that it was his stolen horse, and Martha can't remember his name other than his first name was Jason," Elizabeth answered, rushing her words again, but Fredrick could catch what she was saying this time.

"What did he look like?" Fredrick asked, trying really hard not to sound like a frightened little boy.

"I wasn't there, my husband told me about what happened," Martha answered. "That's why he stayed home and sent me here, so Jason wouldn't make the connection as easily if he saw me here."

"Okay, it's probably safest for everybody if I stay just walk back across to the tomb that I crawled out of. If he does come search the house, I won't be in it, and I can't see him searching the whole tombs, that would just be a waste of time," Fredrick answered. "And I doubt he even knows where they are."

"But what about on the way there? And what about you?" Elizabeth asked, the tears now flowing down her cheeks.

"I'll be okay," Fredrick answered, trying to believe it himself. "If he does catch me, well then, I've lived as a slave once, I can do it again."

"He'll kill you, and what about us?" She demanded.

"Get away from me, go back to the house, pretend like it's just another day. Don't forget to pray."

"You can pray right now," She whispered. In answer Fredrick closed his eyes, and prayed quietly out loud.

"Lord, you are in total control, I used to wonder how an all loving God could let bad things happen, now I know that people sin, and you give us free will, everything you do works together for the good of those who love you. Even if we can't understand it right away, we know that you are in control, and that nothing is going to happen unless you know it'll work out for your good. Even if nothing good comes out of it that we can see, we know that you are great and in control. Help us to trust you, and Lord, please keep everybody safe. Amen."

"Amen." Elizabeth repeated.

"Now seriously, get away from me," Fredrick ordered, Elizabeth nodded, then turned and ran off, with Martha following behind her. He glanced across the field where Mathew and Aaron were, seemingly not having noticed the visit from the two girls, and jogged over to them to tell them the bad news, and the plan.

"You can't just hide in the tomb, it's almost three kilometres away, and there isn't any place to hide on the way! Your almost certain to be caught Fredrick!" Mathew argued when he heard the plan.

"I'd rather be caught alone then with you, or anyone in your family," Fredrick shrugged.

"But you're way less likely to be caught if you just walk to the house, I don't know what you said to Elizabeth to calm her down, but you're not fooling me," Mathew continued.

"I don't care if we get caught! I can't bear the thought of you leaving in chains," Aaron begged.

Looking into his eyes, Fredrick found that for the first time, he actually did look like he was thirteen, and he found himself believing that Aaron actually meant it when he said he thought of him as an older brother. Fredrick stared at him, and it sank in how much he really cared for this kid.

"I care if you're caught," Fredrick told him gently. "I'm not going to the house, and if I make it to the tomb, I'm basically home free."

"I remember when you first showed up, you wouldn't have even bothered to say your opinion, but would've just gone into the house," Mathew sighed. "I could easily count every one of your bruised ribs, and it was easy to tell that even the simplest tasks were hard for you to do, you were so weak. Your master broke your spirit, and nearly killed your body. I don't want you to go back, and walking in the wide open dessert for three kilometres, your capture is almost certain."

"You, and your family, were the ones who brought me back to health. You loved me, and gave me the tools to rebuild my spirit, and you told me about the one who could literally give me a whole new life," Fredrick answered. "Thank-you for opening your home to me, and for following the laws of God before the laws of the government, and in doing so loved me with a love that can only come from God. Yet, there is nothing more you can do for me. I'm going to the tomb."

"I love you," Aaron sighed, hugging him, obviously realizing that they couldn't win this fight. With a start Fredrick realized it was the first time he had hugged him or said that he loved him.

"C'mon buddy, my fate isn't sealed yet," Fredrick sighed, briefly hugging him back. "Don't worry, I'm tough."

"You look really different then you did ten months ago," Aaron pointed out.

"Exactly, he so won't even recognize me. Now go on, act like it's a normal day. If he asks you about me, answer with a bored expression, and act like you don't know," Fredrick told him. Aaron nodded and took a deep breath, and Fredrick got the feeling that he was trying not to cry. Fredrick glanced over at Mathew and looked him square in the eye. "You aren't going to win this argument."

"I see that," Mathew sighed rubbing the back of his neck. Fredrick nodded and was about start towards the tomb, when he stopped and looked at Mathew.

"You're the first Father I've had in eight years, and you've had just as much, if not more of an impact on me as the first one," He told him.

"Fredrick," Mathew sighed. "Walk, don't run, act like you're going for a leisurely stroll, that will be less suspicious."

"Okay," Fredrick nodded, then turned on his heels and walked away.

\*\*\*

Martha studied her best friend, who was in the midst of a massive panic attack, then over at her Mother in law who was also studying her daughter, finishing up the bread that Elizabeth had seemed to forgotten all about.

"When did that happen?" Martha blurted.

"When did what happen?" Elizabeth demanded.

"You, and the boy, last I checked, you're sixteen, and this is the first time you liked a boy." Martha shrugged. "C'mon Eliz, what is your relationship with Fredrick like?"

"How can you even talk like that? Fredrick is about to be brought back to slavery in chains and you're wondering what our relationship is like?"

"Hey girls, c'mon, I think Elizabeth and Martha need to talk without anyone listening, and we need to get rid of Fredrick's stuff," She announced.

"What happens to runaway slaves if they're caught?" Elizabeth asked in almost a whisper once her family was gone.

"Do you really want to know?" Martha sighed, putting her arm around Elizabeth's shoulders.

"Yes, no, I don't know," Elizabeth muttered.

"Do you wanna come to my house? I need to head back there, I've never left Andrew alone with Mary-Liz and Jonathan for this long before, and my family needs supper, but I really don't want to leave you alone," Martha explained. "Plus, Jonathan still won't eat real food..."

"Okay, that's funny," Elizabeth laughed, with tears still painting her cheeks, imagining her brother home alone with his six month old crying son, who wouldn't be soothed for anything. "Yeah, we can go to your house."

She ran up the stairs to inform her Mother of their plans, then wrapped her shawl around her arms and followed her sister-in-law who was already ready and waiting.

"You know, this is kind of nice, just the two of us again," Elizabeth commented crossing her arms in the quickly cooling air.

"What do you mean?" Martha asked.

"Like when we were kids, and we used to play together, and we'd talk for hours," Elizabeth sighed. "But no more."

"I am a wife and Mother Eliz," Martha shrugged.

"Yeah, but we stopped talking long before then." Elizabeth sighed. "I know it was only expected, but I still miss it."

"We grew apart," Martha agreed. "I married when I was fifteen and was a mother when I was sixteen. Are you ready for marriage? It's a huge commitment, especially with your lover, where is he gonna go if he's free?"

"I don't wanna talk about it," she answered honestly. "And we aren't lovers, we're friends, although to answer your question, I don't think *he* knows what he wants to do with freedom."

# CHAPTER 10

"*I'm busted,*" Fredrick moaned inwardly, not daring to make a sound out loud. He could see Jason from the corner of his eye, he could only look away, and try not to draw attention to himself. Part of him prayed harder than ever before, and another part of him forced himself to remember Mathew's words to walk and not run.

He glanced at the ground, and raised his hand, as if playing with his hair, to hide his face. Two thirds of the way there, he only had about a kilometre left to go, and he was almost sure he wasn't going to make it.

"That's him over there!" Jason Cummings voice yelled, and Fredrick couldn't have fought the will to run if he tried, but he pushed himself as hard as he could. He could here footsteps chasing him, but he dared not look behind him for fear of slowing down. He could feel his lungs set on fire, and he started to see black dots. Even though he had grown a lot stronger in the past few months, he knew he was by no means strong, or healthy. He couldn't run like this forever, and the men chasing him could diffidently go longer then he could. He ducked behind a hill, hoping to buy himself at least enough time to catch his breath. No such luck.

"I think he went down here," An unidentified voice, that was way too close for comfort, announced. Fredrick plugged his nose, unable to suppress the panting by mere willpower, the fire in his lungs spreading to his throat and head, but he ignored it.

*God*, he thought, to scared and desperate for air to actually form a full prayer. He hoped that would be enough.

"Found him," The voice announced, at the exact same moment that a hand grabbed his arm. Fredrick half screamed, half sucked in as much oxygen as he could, and immediately started struggling. He blindly kneed the slave catcher in the groin. While the slave catcher was busy yelping in pain, Fredrick turned around and ran, strait into another slave catcher. This one grabbed his wrists, turned him around, wrapped his arms around his torso and held him so he couldn't move his arms, and could barely move his legs higher than the man shins. It didn't matter how hard he kicked them though, it was like his shins were made of steel.

*"I don't care! I'm done being a slave, and I have way to many people who care about me now to just give up!"* Fredrick thought, and put as much strength as he could muster into kicking the man's shins. The man groaned, not from pain, but from annoyance as if Fredrick was an insect, that was just a minor inconvenience in his life, and kicked him in the back of his knee, a move that would've crumbled him to the ground if he wasn't lashed in human chains.

"Yeah, I've always preferred the ones who try to fight anyway, they're so much more fun!" The man holding Fredrick laughed.

"You're strong!" The first guy complained. Fredrick, panting, looked up at him for the first time and couldn't believe his eyes. The boy in front of him was his age. He was skinny as if he didn't get enough to eat, his one eye had a bruise underneath it, and he partly wondered if he had looked like that when he had first runaway, but he quickly decided against it. This guy didn't eat enough, but he wasn't starving, and he didn't look like he was as abused as Fredrick was, but he was probably still a slave. His clothes were worn and torn, and his blonde hair fell over his large hazel eyes, but before he could figure out where he had seen eyes like that before, an all too familiar voice came around the corner.

"I have been looking for you for almost a year!" Jason Cummings voice growled coming around the outhouse. "You are in so much trouble!"

"And that... year... was the best.... of my life!" Fredrick sassed, still gasping for air. He probably should've stayed silent, but he figured he couldn't get into any more trouble. And besides he was too short of oxygen to actually feel anything, so it wasn't until after he caught his breath that he realized there was blood pouring down his chin from his nose.

"He has quite the mind of his own, doesn't he?" the boy commented and Fredrick suspected he was still holding a grudge from when Fredrick kicked him. The boy studied him like he was a fascinating specimen in a museum.

"He knows what happens to runaway slaves who are caught, he's as good dead this one." The man holding him captive laughed.

*Okay, has anyone ever told you that you have a sick sense of humour?* Fredrick thought, not bothering to say it out loud.

"Hey Johnson, do you think he could survive, like, fifteen to twenty lashes? I want to take him home and whip him to death in front of the rest of my slaves, but it doesn't seem right to save the whole punishment till then," Jason asked, hearing his plan, Fredrick resumed struggling, he had more people than ever before in his life who cared about what was going to happen, now, of all times, he did not want to die especially murdered in front of his sister.

"Oh probably, he's strong." Johnson shrugged. "Frankly, if we're going to whip him, I'd rather we do it here, if he's wounded he'll be more compliant, and even if he passes out, I'd rather carry a passed out slave, then drag one who's desperate to regain his taste of freedom. However, I'm going to ask you not to take him back until we figure out who was harbouring him."

"Sounds like a deal, I'll bring him back as soon as the trial is over. I'll get the whip, you two get his shirt off." Jason shrugged.

"No!" Fredrick moaned, just before being shoved into the dirt. Both the boy, and the Johnson guy, who was had brown hair and eyes, was freakishly tall, strong, and overall looked intimidating, stood on either side of him, so even if he tried to run away, he couldn't have gotten far.

"Take your shirt off," Johnson ordered. Fredrick looked up at him, feeling way more intimidated by the man now that he could see him, and almost subconsciously obeyed. No wonder he couldn't get free from his grasp, he must've felt like a struggling aphid. Fredrick shivered, trying to come up with an escape plan, but both pairs of eyes bore into him, and he really couldn't think of anything that wouldn't result him collecting bruises.

"Alright, do you two wanna hold him?" Jason asked holding a whip in one hand. Fredrick groaned, but didn't even bother struggling as Johnson and the boy pulled him to his feet. All of the marks on his back had healed to nothing more than scars, and here he was about to get them all back! At least the blonde had the common courtesy to look reluctant.

The first lash surprised him, somehow he had forgotten the pain, and he yelped. Refusing to yelp again he bit his lip and only grunted for the second one. They kept coming, until eventually it felt like his whole back was on fire, and didn't even have the strength to yelp in pain anyway.

He would've collapsed from pain, had it not been for the slave catchers holding him up. He was dimly aware that he had begun to whimper, but who cared? The pain was excruciating, and he didn't care enough to pretend otherwise.

"*God, help,*" he mouthed, though he was pretty sure that no sounds came out. That's when everything went black.

\*\*\*

"God's in control Eliz," Andrew told her bouncing his two year old on his knees. Elizabeth had volunteered to make supper while Martha nursed Jonathan, and Andrew did his best to keep Mary-Liz from crying. She didn't know what was wrong obviously, but she could tell from the way her parents and aunt were acting that something wasn't right, and it was clearly stressing her out.

"Are you gonna be okay?" Elizabeth asked, looking up from the mashed potato she was making. "You were caught with his horse."

"I don't know," Andrew sighed looking down at Mary-Liz whose blonde curls bounced along with his knee. The sight caused him to half smile, and then the smile dropped, and he got a serious look on his face again. "I honestly don't know."

"God promises to never leave us, nor forsake us," Elizabeth reminded her brother.

"I know, but that doesn't mean bad things won't happen, it just means that God is going to be there when they do happen," Andrew answered. He looked down at Mary-Liz again and spoke as if to her, but his words were directed to Elizabeth. "I'm worried about them, if something happens to me, what's gonna happen to them? It would be one thing if I'm just going to die, but I won't, I'll leave behind a widow and three fatherless children."

"Three?" Elizabeth asked.

"She's four weeks," Andrew whispered. Elizabeth blinked and stared at her brother, Martha was four weeks pregnant? Of all times, now? "If I die now, I'm never even gonna get to see him. Jonathan's not going to remember me, and Mary-Liz will likely forget me sooner or later. My children will know me only by stories. Martha will have to find a way to feed them without me. She'll be a maid in a rich man's home, or she'll rent out the bedroom and live off of the money from the rent. All this of course with three children. She won't be able to send them to school, she'll have to find time to teach them herself, or they'll grow up illiterate, and be forever poor."

Elizabeth studied her older brother. He had been the hero of her childhood, and if she was honest, he still was. He had been the one who taught her how to play hide and seek, he had helped her catch her first frog at the oasis, he had held her hand when he took her to school the first time, and had helped her with her homework in the years to come.

He had always seemed impenetrable. Nothing would ever be able to break him. To Elizabeth's surprise, she realized her big, tough older brother, was scared, terrified even. He was terrified as to what would happen to himself, but almost more than that, he was scared about what was going to happen to the family he was leaving behind.

"That's why you took the horse in the first place," Elizabeth gasped, finally connecting the dots. "Because you loved us, and wanted to protect us."

"Yeah," Andrew answered, seemingly confused as to why that wasn't obvious. Honestly, Elizabeth couldn't figure out why that wasn't obvious either. She walked over and hugged him, remembering for the first time in a long time why he was her favourite brother the whole time she was growing up, and over all her favourite person.

"I love you too," Elizabeth told him. "And I know I'm just a girl, but I won't let Martha walk the road of widowhood alone. Nothings sealed yet anyway, there's still hope. Besides, with the rate I'm going, I'm going to be an old maid."

"You're not an old maid Eliz, you're still sixteen and beautiful," Andrew told her.

"Almost seventeen, and the only person who's ever liked me is either on the run from, or caught, by slave catchers," Elizabeth corrected.

"Wait, the slave boy liked you?" Andrew demanded.

"Don't tell your wife," Elizabeth ordered.

"Aunt Wizabeth," Mary-Liz announced looking up at her, leaning against her father's chest. "I like you too!"

"Aw, I like you too, Mary-Liz," Elizabeth smiled.

"You tell her Mary, don't give up on yourself yet Eliz," Andrew agreed.

"Yeah!" Mary-Liz grinned.

"Oh right, Supper!" Elizabeth suddenly exclaimed running to the hearth.

"And that is why Aunt Elizabeth and Mama were friends for so long, neither of them can cook," Andrew explained to his daughter, who giggled.

"I heard that," Martha remarked coming out of the bedroom, with Jonathan on her hip.

"What?" Andrew asked innocently as Martha kissed him on the top of his head.

"You know exactly what," Martha groaned. Andrew smiled and deviously gave the two year old on his lap a high five. "Here, do you wanna hold Jonathan?"

"Sure," Andrew nodded as Martha placed Jonathan on his free lap. "Do you feel better now that you've eaten buddy?" Jonathan nodded and joined his sister in resting his head on their Father's chest. "They're tired."

"Yeah, well Mary-Liz woke up early from her nap, and proceeded to wake her brother up," Martha agreed taking a moment to observe the scene of her husband and children cuddling, then set the table.

"Supper's ready," Elizabeth commented looking up from the hearth.

"How burnt is it?" Andrew teased.

"It's not burnt!" Elizabeth groaned.

"Whatever you say sis," Andrew teased. "Um, as much as I like to, I don't really don't see how I'm gonna be eating a whole meal holding two children."

"C'mere Mary." Martha smiled, transferring her from her Father's lap to a highchair right next to him. "Are you good with Jonathan?"

"Yeah, I can do one kid, I just can't do two," Andrew answered standing the baby up on his lap, who immediately started bouncing up and down. Andrew obliged and bounced his knees up and down, holding Jonathan by the waist to steady him, as Jonathan giggled with delight. Martha stared at them for a moment and then helped Elizabeth set the table and bring the food out.

It was halfway through the meal when the inevitable happened. There was a knock on the door, and Martha and Andrew just looked at each other for a moment, then both stood up at the exact same time.

"No," Martha whimpered backing against the wall, hugging her torso. "No!"

"Martha..." Andrew began standing up and holding the baby in his arms. Martha didn't seem to hear him, and Andrew looked perplexed, when the knock came again, this time more urgently, Andrew had no choice but to open the door.

There was two men in the door, both were really strong, one with brown hair and eyes, and another with thinning grey hair, and hazel-green eyes. Elizabeth stood up and walked over as if in a dream, while Martha was still busy whimpering in the corner.

"Andrew, we found him, he's obviously been hidden by someone and you're our top suspect," the strong man explained. "Even if it wasn't you, it's pretty obvious that you assisted in helping a runaway slave some way or another."

"Take Jonathan," Andrew whispered handing Elizabeth the baby, who immediately started crying, sensing something was wrong. Turning back to the men he added, "Please, not in front of them, I'll go with you." With that Andrew and the men left the house, leaving Elizabeth unsure what to do with her shocked sister-in-law and crying nephew.

***

Fredrick woke up, feeling dazed. He was laying on his back, on a hard, wood, floor. His head hurt, but the minute he moved, even an inch, sharp pain rippled up his back and he groaned.

"Sleeping beauty awakes," the boy that had found him commented, sounding bored, although Fredrick couldn't actually see him from where he lay. Decided to ignore his prison guard, Fredrick struggled to get off his back. As soon as he tried to roll over though, he found that one of his wrists was chained the post of... a bed?

"Where are we?" Fredrick moaned, still painfully trying to get off his back. He was pressed against the side of the bed, and he couldn't roll over without scraping his back on the floor. Despite everything, he had to admit whoever put him here was really good at maximizing pain...

"In town, hotel specifically," he shrugged. "And, I'm not supposed to let you talk unless spoken too. Do you need help?"

"I think you've helped me enough – OW!" Fredrick snapped, finally succeeding in pulling himself off of his back and into a sitting position.

Once up, he could looked around the room. The bed he was chained to was the only bed in there. The boy sat at an expensive looking table with an ashtray in the centre of it, full of ashes and cigar butts. The floor was oak wood, and a window was right across from Fredrick, beside that was an elaborate dresser. He didn't bother looking behind him, but he assumed the door was back there.

"Your back looks terrible," the boy said, glancing over at him briefly before going back to the ashtray, which really couldn't be that entertaining.

"Thank you," Fredrick snapped sarcastically. "You have no idea what it feels like to be whipped, why do you think I ran away in the first place?"

"I know what it feels like, I'm a slave too, you know." he rolled his eyes. "I just never ran away from my master."

"Sorry," Fredrick muttered. "I had perilous circumstances that prompted me to take drastic measures."

"I don't think I've ever heard a slave boy use words like that before," The boy laughed. "Fredrick right?"

"Yep, and your name?" Fredrick asked.

"My name is Mathew Couring, most everyone calls me Matt though," He answered looking over at him. After a pause he continued. "He was the one hiding you, wasn't he? My father, and

82

Andrew's father?" Fredrick made no reply to that, but Matt shrugged like he wasn't that surprised and the matter was settled. "Small world. I guess I can see them doing something that stupid in the name of love."

"If they're so loving, why don't you just go home?" Fredrick asked.

"I don't know, and it's none of your business anyway," Matt snapped. Fredrick answered that by darting his eyes to the floor. "Sorry, but trust me when I say they don't want me back now. Besides, Steven will actually look for me if I run away from him."

"They looked too Matt," Fredrick told him softly. "Elizabeth said the day you ran away, your Pa and Andrew didn't get home until two in the morning, and they were up at six to look for you. She said Andrew and your Pa searched without stopping for two weeks, and your Pa searched every night for three months. Nobody could find any trace of you."

"Well, I did arrange a job with a travelling caravan before I even ranaway, I was gone for like six months. Then I squandered my wealth and sold myself to a man who won't let me eat the animal's food, like every good little prodigal should. Still, you would think I would hear about it if he really searched nonstop for me, especially if it was for three months."

Fredrick started to shrug, and decided last minute that was a bad idea, Matt watched him for a moment before standing up. "The second level of a prison is the worst part, that's where all the thieves and murders are, or anyone withholding information. It's also where the living conditions are the worst, and the punishments are the harshest. The only people who take care of them, are slaves, in other words, me. I knew nothing about medical care before I was sold, but I've picked a few things up since then, and anyway, your back needs attention, even if I taught myself everything I know by trial and error. In other words, whether you want medical help or not, you're getting it. I'm actually not that bad."

Fredrick only smiled softly, and leaning sideways against the bedpost while Matt set to work.

# CHAPTER 11

Fredrick stood in the middle of the desert, with nothing around him but sand. There was a girl in the near distance, who could have easily been either Margret or Elizabeth. He started to run to her, but the faster he ran, the farther away from her he got. Finally, exhausted, he collapsed into the sand, panting. He looked up, only to find that she had somehow appeared right in front of him, only the girl was somehow both Elizabeth, and Margret. She moved her lips as if she was talking, but Fredrick couldn't hear a word.

He jumped to his feet and reached his hands out, as if to hug her, but suddenly he wasn't in the desert, but a dungeon, and he was chained to a wall. He couldn't get his hands more than a foot away from the wall. Suddenly the girl changed, and she was only Margret.

"Margret!" Fredrick exclaimed.

"You can't have us both Fredrick, we're from two different worlds," she told him. Then she faded into mist and blew away.

"Wait! Margret! Elizabeth!" Fredrick called after her, but he was just yelling to an empty room, except for, wait... "Father!"

"Fredrick!" Father exclaimed, with that wonderful, strong, safe voice, coming to stand in front of him. His brown hair was neatly trimmed like it always was, his bluish green eyes that normally twinkled with delight, now filled with concern. "What happened?"

"I can't do this! Things were going from bad to worse when you died, now Margret and I are prisoners, and I can't get free!" Fredrick explained, he suddenly felt like crying, in a moment the feeling was gone and was replaced with anger. "I miss you, you were the only thing that was good in my life!"

"Don't get mad at me, I wasn't the only thing good in your life, you had your sister, and now you have the Courings. Do you remember the story I used to tell you and your sister about the king, who came down his kingdom and lived as a poor boy, then was killed by the very people he came to save?" Father asked.

"Yeah, Mathew told me the same story," Fredrick told him. "The king, he died for me, he's my saviour too."

"I heard, I live with him," Father told him, the familiar twinkle filled the bluish green eyes again. "He promised that he's never going to leave or forsake you. He'll always protect you, sometimes bad things happen, but that's because we live in a fallen world. That's why there's death, and sickness, and slavery. But the good news is, that even in our darkest moment, God's always there."

"What about you?" Fredrick asked.

"I'll be waiting to see you on judgement day," Father told him. "Don't despair, lean on God, through the good times and the bad, he likes to be leaned on."

"What's heaven like?" Fredrick asked.

"Well it'll have to wait for you, God still has plans for you. But for conversation's sake, it's beautiful. Actually, beautiful is too normal of a word to describe it. Even stunning, or majestic, just aren't powerful enough words to describe it. You're Mother's there, so is the Courings little boy, but the best part is Jesus, and the pure holiness he radiates. Speaking of which I have to go."

"Wait! Father don't leave me!" Fredrick begged trying to run to him, but he was still chained to the wall.

"I love you," Father told him, then he to, faded into mist, and Fredrick was alone. He felt hollow, like he had lost his Father all over again.

"Somebody!" He called. "Please! Mathew? Elizabeth?" Just then a cold hand gabbed his shoulder and started shaking him, and suddenly he wasn't chained to a wall in a dungeon, but a bedpost in a hotel.

*So basically that same thing, except I'm in a room full of slave catchers, instead of loved ones... I think I'd rather be chained to a wall!* Fredrick thought to himself looking over at Matt, who was the still the only one in the room, so it was kind of obvious he was the one who had woken him.

"You need to work on your habit of talking in your sleep," He ordered. "I just saw them come into the hotel from the window, they'll be here any minute."

Fredrick half wondered who 'they' were until, Jason Cummings and Steven Johnson (Matt's master) walked into the hotel room, and Matt glanced over at them, as if waiting for them to talk, and dreading what they were going to say.

Mr. Johnson knelt over and used a key to unlock the chain around the bedpost, and then chained Fredrick's hands behind his back. When he pulled the newly captured slave to his feet, pain rippled up Fredrick's back but he ignored it, it wasn't nearly as bad now that he wasn't laying on it anyway, and Matt washing it down did actually make it feel better. Then, he was lead to a corner and made to stand in it.

"Whose house were you hiding in?" he demanded. Fredrick stared at the ground and didn't say a word, a fist flew at his eye, but he was defenceless with his hands immobilized behind his back. "I asked you a question Fredrick, whose house were you hiding in?" Fredrick made no sound, instead stared at the ground

"Matt," Mr. Johnson ordered the boy standing in the corner. "Grow a backbone and get over here."

"What am I supposed to do?" Matt asked.

"Well, you can work on channelling your anger instead of bottling it up," Steven suggested.

"I don't have anger to channel," Matt answered, sounding like he was offended.

"Everybody has anger," Steven contradicted. "C'mere and hit him."

"Um..." Matt began, looking like he really didn't want to hit Fredrick, but came over to the corner anyway.

"Look at you, and look at me, either you beat him or I beat him," Steven told him.

Matt groaned and slapped Fredrick's cheek with the back of his hand. It didn't really hurt compared to his eye, or back, but for the sake of the audience he did his best to make it look like it did. Unfortunately Steven saw right through it and shoved Matt into Fredrick. That actually did hurt, and both of them grunted simultaneously.

"Do you want to join your friends in prison? Or even join him in being beaten mercilessly, 'cause I can arrange both. When I say hit someone, you hit him, hard, got it?" Steven snapped.

"Got it," Matt muttered avoiding his gaze.

"Good," Steven answered. "Now try again."

Matt sighed and looked back at Fredrick, with a look that said "if I beat you, will you promise not to betray my father?" Fredrick actually felt so bad for him he wished Steven would just beat him, even though he was about three times as big as Matt, and almost that much bigger then Fredrick.

"Close your eyes, and imagine I'm someone you hate," Fredrick suggested. He turned to Steven and said it as a taunt but he meant it as a promise to Matt. "Besides, it doesn't matter anyway, 'cause there is nothing anyone can do to me that will make me talk."

"We'll see, everyone has a breaking point," Steven answered, his face calm and unreadable. "Now Matt." Matt nodded and closed his eyes, obviously Fredrick's advice worked, cause the next thing he knew pain exploded in his lower lip, and he was pretty sure Matt had split it, but he managed not to make a sound. Matt made the mistake of opening his eyes, saw his lip, and literally paled.

"Either you beat him with your fists, or with a whip, go again," Steven ordered.

"Please don't make me do this," Matt begged.

"Your choice, fists or a whip," Steven snapped

"Please just use your fists," Fredrick begged in the corner. Matt sighed and punched him in the centre of his chest. Fredrick couldn't help but grunt, but Matt somehow managed to close his eyes and ignore him, and didn't stop until Steven ordered him too.

"Whose house were you hiding in?" Steven demanded. When Fredrick didn't say anything Steven shoved Matt out of the way, and started pounding on his chest, hard. Although it wasn't until Fredrick heard one of his ribs crack that he sank to the ground, where Steven started kicking him.

"Okay," Jason Cummings interrupted. "He's had enough." Fredrick stood up, as quick as he could considering his hands were cuffed behind his back, and he was now bloody, bruised, and probably broken. Steven glared at him as if the last thing in the world he wanted was to stop beating him.

*"God promised, that he's never going to leave or forsake you. He'll always protect you, sometimes bad things happen, but that's because we live in a fallen world. That's why there's death, and sickness, and slavery. But the good news is, that even in our darkest moment, God's always there,"* His Father's voice came to him, followed shortly by one of the first things Mathew had said to him. *"Christianity is about loving your neighbour, doing good to those who do evil, praying for those who rise up against you, forgiving those who do you wrong cause ultimately that's what Christ did for us. 'While we were still sinners, Christ died for us.' Christianity is about learning to love others, even those, especially those, who don't deserve it."*

*So God, what I'm getting here is that you're right here watching this, and you want me to forgive them?* Fredrick demanded looking around the room. There was Jason Cummings, who had murdered his Father and enslaved both himself and his sister. Then there was Steven, who had just spent who knew how long trying to get Fredrick to betray the only family he had. *God, you expect me to forgive these people? They're horrible!*

Even as he thought all that, he couldn't help but realize the truth. If they weren't horrible, they wouldn't need forgiveness. He needed forgiveness. He had allowed his anger to fester in his soul for far too long. It was time to release it.

*Lord, I don't know how to live without anger, it's what keeps me going. It's like a security blanket. I don't even think I* want *to give it up. Help me to want to give up my anger, help me to want to forgive, even those who don't deserve it, 'cause I know they're the ones who need it,* Fredrick prayed. Blood poured down his chin, and both his lip and his nose hurt, so he couldn't tell what it was from, his hands were still cuffed so he couldn't wipe the blood away. He could feel the eye Steven punched started to swelling, and his ribs were so bruised it hurt to breathe, but he hardly noticed it. The anger was what he lived by. Underneath the anger was what? If he let it go, what would happen?

"So Fredrick," Mr. Johnson began, grabbing him by the hair. "Do you wanna go for a brief recess and then do the whole thing over again, or do wanna tell me right now who was hiding you?"

"Who said someone was hiding me?" Fredrick taunted glaring at the floor.

"You don't get that fat living on the streets," Mr. Johnson argued. "Was it Andrew?"

"I swear, I don't even know him," Fredrick answered.

"Suit yourself." Mr. Johnson laughed. "Matt, chain him back to the bed, and Fredrick, I do have Andrew. Your willpower, however sweet, may be futile."

Fredrick growled as Matt unclasped one of his wrists, and chained him to the bed with shaky hands. To live a life without anger was truly beyond his comprehension...

\*\*\*

Andrew wrapped his arms around his legs, and shivered. So this is what the second level of a prison looked like. He had seen the first level before, through a window with bars on it, he thought it looked terrible. Now, he thought it looked like paradise. He was locked in a cell so small he couldn't even stretch out when he lay down, and a chain clasped around his wrist attached him to the wall. It was dark, so dark he could barely see his hand waving in front of his face, and he couldn't see into the other cells. He wasn't sure whether to be disgusted that he was used to the smell or not, and he was pretty sure prison guards were allowed to torture prisoners withholding information.

Andrew sighed and rested his head on his knees. Things could be worse, and he wasn't the first guy to land in prison for just doing what God called him to do. Honestly, Paul was in prison how many times? Actually all the apostles ended up in prison a lot. Peter was released from prison by an angel, and wasn't it Paul and Silas who were in prison when there was a huge earthquake then all the doors opened, and the shackles fell off the prisoners?

*"Yeah, God can save me from prison, but I'm not betting on it,"* Andrew thought. *"And besides, the majority of the time the apostles weren't saved at all. And Jesus did die for me, going to prison for following his commands is the least I can do…"*

"God," Andrew whispered into his knees. "I don't think I'm quite in the place that I can say thank-you for counting me worthy of suffering for your name, but I'll follow you wherever you lead me. Even in prison, I pray that I can be a light for you. And Lord, if it's not too much to ask, please keep my family safe." There was silence in the prison for a while, and Andrew didn't even notice the man that had arrested him, Steven Johnson or whatever, show up until he was unlocking the door.

"So, you had the horse, who had the boy?" he asked standing over him.

"What if I don't know?" Andrew muttered. The man laughed heartily, a cruel laugh, that enjoyed others pain.

"Oh, I don't fall for that Andrew, I know you know. I also know even you aren't stupid enough to keep both the runaway and his horse," Steven told him. "Besides, I can enjoy beating you even more then the last person I tried to get answers out of. You don't have a master who's determined that you'll live long enough to be made an example out of. You can just die in prison."

"I already told you, I got the horse in a fair deal!" Andrew begged.

"Who did you get it from?" Steven demanded.

"I don't know, I had never met him before," Andrew answered.

"You know Christian, lying is a sin," Steven told him. Andrew didn't reply to that, because he didn't know how. He wasn't his Father, Mathew was the perfect Christian. Andrew did his best, but he always managed to fall short.

"Andrew! Answer me!" Steven ordered slapping his face.

"*God! I don't know what I'm doing!*" Andrew thought. "*I need you.*"

"Where did you get the horse?" Steven ordered. It was worded like a question, but it sounded like an order. An order to give his father up. His foot dove into Andrew's shin and he yelped.

"*Oh that you would keep silent, and it would be your wisdom,*" *Job 13:5,* The verse popped into Andrew's head from nowhere, but he decided to listen.

"So? Who had the boy?" Steven demanded. There was silence for a moment and then the man shoved him so hard Andrew could hear his rib crack. He groaned and tried to sink back to the ground but Steven held him up. "To give you a forewarning, I've already gone through this whole thing already. I'm annoyed. You will not be getting any sympathy from me. Who hid the slave?"

"Andrew!" Steven yelled shoving his broken ribcage so hard tears stung his eyes, and he was pretty sure Steven just broke another rib. Steven growled, and switched from prolonged punching to rapid fire, then back to the slow torture. Finally after about an hour he grabbed his throat, and squeezed. Andrew didn't care, if he died in the name of love there were few greater honours. Just before Andrew blacked out Steven dropped his grip and Andrew dropped to the ground. Too sore to breathe, to oxygen deprived not to gasp, he sat on his knees and unshackled hand, in complete misery.

"Speak," Steven ordered. Andrew ignored him, and focused on trying to get oxygen back into his lungs with minimum pain. Steven groaned and kneed his ribcage which resulted in nothing more than Andrew whimpering and collapsing (painfully) on the ground. His shackled wrist slightly above his head, his unshackled hand cradling his broken ribs.

"Well, you're tough," Steven decided. "Let's see, this time tomorrow we'll meet? Same place?" Andrew groaned in answer as Steven left and locked the door behind him

"Just tell him, he gonna find out eventually, and his techniques of getting information out of you are only gonna get more cruel and painful," the prisoner across from him whispered. Andrew painfully sat up and looked across at the skinny prisoner that he could only see a shadow of because it was so dark.

"I'm not telling him anything," Andrew whispered back.

"Then good luck," He whispered, just then the guard walked through again and the man held his tongue until he passed. "Gotta be careful of the man, he beats anyone who says a word, but he checks on us in a routine ten minutes, so if you can remember when he last checked on you, your usually fine to talk in low volumes. For the record, helping a slave is probably the most admirable way you can land down here."

"Um... thank-you," Andrew whispered, unsure exactly what that was supposed to mean.

"Seriously," the man whispered. "I hope you don't regret it."

"He was caught, my attempts were futile," Andrew pointed out. "And I didn't do it to protect him."

"But he was free for a while, and like I said, your still one of the most admirable people down here. Don't underestimate the power of a short while of freedom though," The man whispered. "I'm David by the way."

"Andrew," he whispered in reply.

# CHAPTER 12

"How do you break him Matt?" Steven demanded walking into the barn where Matt was busy grooming one of Steven's horses.

"Fredrick?" Matt asked looking up. "I don't know, I met him the same day you did."

"Not him, your brother," Steven snapped.

"Andrew? I haven't seen him in over a year, how am I supposed to know what his breaking point is?" Matt sighed staring at the wall.

"I dunno, guess, it can't be that different from what it was a year ago!" Steven yelled, and Matt slightly cowered at Steven's anger. Steven groaned, pulled him out of the stall, and shoved him against the stall door opposite of the one he was working in. Which basically scared both horses more then it scared Matt. "You have literally five seconds to talk before I pull out the whip."

"I seriously don't know, he was like the hero of my youth, I don't know if he has a weakness!" Matt answered quickly, 90% certain that answer wasn't going to cut it.

"Have you ever seen him cry?" Steven demanded.

"Yes," Matt answered, raking his brain for an example. "He cried more when we were kids obviously, but I don't know, since we were little kids... He cried at our little brother's funeral."

"Anybody would cry for that, keep talking," Steven ordered.

"He doesn't cry in front of people very often," Matt raising his hands in self-defence.

"He's just like you," Steven decided.

"What does that mean?" Matt demanded.

"It means forcing him to watch others pain, or forcing him to cause someone else pain, is way better torture then physically hurting him," Steven answered. "The hero of your youth, you're just like him."

***

Andrew sighed, then winced and leaned against the wall. "Why can't I die again?"

"Oh please, you've been down here for a day, you can't die now," David lectured him. "Remember, breathe deeply or your lungs will collapse from lack of use. Now do it again." Andrew suppressed a groan and took another deep breath, which was stopped by a bunch of painful coughs.

"Very good," David teased. "Coughing is good for you too."

"Ugh, I feel so gross, and he's coming back!" Andrew complained. "I don't know what he's going to do this time, it could be worse."

"Shhh!" David ordered, just as the guard walked by. Once he'd gone David spoke again. "Do you have family?"

"What does that have to do with anything?" Andrew asked miserably.

"They give you reason to live," Someone else explained. "Reason to fight for another day. If you don't have family, do you have friends?"

"I have family," Andrew answered. "A wife and two kids, another on the way."

"That's wonderful," David reminded him. "Tell me about them."

"Mary-Liz, the greatest day of my life was the day she was born. The first time she smiled, she smiled at me. Every time I would come home, she'd run to greet me at the door. 'Papa's home!' She'd cry.

94

I'd hold out my hands and she'd run into my arms. I'd swing her around, her pretty blonde curls bouncing down her back.

"Jonathan is the cute one. He loves to be bounced around, he's six months old and he's happiest when he's being tossed or something. He crawls around the house following his sister. He's such a bubbly baby, always full of smiles. If he can get Martha or I to hold his hands, he'll be perfectly content to walk around the house for hours. He's a little adventurer that one.

"Martha... There's nothing to say, she's the love of my life. She listens when I have a problem, I don't deserve her. The only time she's not on her knees in prayer is when she's serving those around her. I often wonder how she does it. I tease her sometimes 'cause she always forgets about supper and burns it, but honestly if I did everything she did I'd probably forget to make supper. Before I was arrested, she left me to babysit for about an hour. An hour. By the time she came back the house was a mess. Mary-Liz had almost torn our family bible to shreds before I interceded, and in classic two year old fashion, threw a massive temper tantrum. Her crying got Jonathan started, and... yeah, that woman is amazing."

"That's good Andrew," David told him. "Think about that when you're low, not about your broken bones."

"What about you?" Andrew asked. "Do you have family?"

"Yeah, I've got a wife and five kids. The oldest would be fourteen if my math is correct," David answered. He proceeded to tell Andrew about each of them, stopping halfway through when footsteps came ahead of time with a slight gasp of fear.

"Hey Andrew," Steven greeted unlocking his cell door, sounding like he was faking being apologetic, which just made Andrew more nervous. "We got off on a rough start yesterday. I'm sorry about that, I lost my temper, can you forgive me? Alright, you don't have to say anything, it's just... I heard about Johnny. Your little brother who died about a year and a half ago right? You named your son after him didn't you? I seem to remember you saying that woman in your house "take Jonathan" right before you handed her a baby, that was your son right?"

"What are doing?" Andrew asked, because he was scaring him the way he was wording everything.

"Do you miss your son? Do you wanna see him again?" Steven asked.

"You can't take a child from his Mother," Andrew argued.

"Oh your right, maybe I should just take your whole family? I'm sure they miss you just as much as you miss them," Steven told him. "Your children can watch as I flog their Mother in front of their Father who will do what again? Oh right, nothing, 'cause you're not going to say who was hiding the slave. Still not going to speak? Would you rather I rip your unborn child out of her womb first before I flog her?"

"Stop!" Andrew begged.

"Andrew he can't do that, he needs reasons before he hurts anyone. He can't hurt someone because of what their husband or Father does," David objected.

"James! Get in here!" Steven yelled. A minute later the guard who patrolled that section of the prison ran over and Steven ordered him to take David off somewhere to be flogged. As David was led away, Andrew saw him as more than a shadow for the first time. He was thin, as thin as the slave boy was when he was found, and just as abused. *"He's either a runaway slave, or an escaped prisoner. Although, he's too tanned to be from a prison."* Those were Andrew's exact words... They were all too true. Two big differences marked them. David was pale, almost no colour to his face, and he had courage. Fredrick had cowered against a wall in a room full of people who would never lay a finger on him, David was being led away to be flogged, and he had a streak of noble defiance in his eyes.

"Idiot," Steven scoffed. "I'm the head prison guard, owner of the only person to take care of the second level prisoner, and overseer of all the trials. Any sane man would follow the rules around me. Whatever, so he has a point. I still have more though. I heard your other brother ran away after Johnny died right? Matt? Do you miss him? Lie awake at night wondering if he's being torn apart by Jackals at that very moment?"

"What are you getting at this time?" Andrew sighed.

"He's a good slave, good hard worker," Steven explained.

"Wait, Matt..." Andrew began then stopped, his brain working a hundred miles faster than his mouth could form words.

"What? You haven't met the doctor of the second level yet?" Steven laughed. "If you haven't met him yet, you'll meet him later."

"What are you talking about?" Andrew demanded.

"All the prisoners on this level love him. Hold on, I'll be right back," Steven answered locking the cell door behind him as he left.

"Matt's your brother?" someone whispered but Andrew ignored him, and waited in tense silence until the door unlocked, and sure enough, his little brother got thrown onto the floor in front of him.

"Matt," Andrew gasped. Matt gasped and averted his eyes away from him as if his biggest fear was facing him. Steven grabbed Matt's hair, which must've been at least two inches longer then last time Andrew saw him, and lifted his head so Matt was forced to face Andrew.

"Do you still love him? Even after he ran away?" Steven asked.

"Please don't hurt him," Andrew whispered.

"Are you going to tell me who hid the slave?" Steven asked. Andrew fell silent, hesitating, a moment to long apparently cause Steven unhooked a whip from his belt and slashed it across Matt's back, who grunted, but other than that he made no sound.

"He didn't even do anything!" One of the prisoners from another cell objected.

"Shut up," Steven ordered the other prisoner lashing Matt across the back again. "What about you Andrew? Do you have anything to say?" There was a brief pause, then came another crack of the whip, and a grunt from Matt.

"Okay stop, I'll tell you!" Andrew objected.

"No Andrew! Don't!" Matt yelled, then grunted as another lash went across his back. "It was my Father. My Father hid Fredrick."

"You knew?" Steven demanded pulling him up by his hair and slamming his scarred back against the cold, brick wall. Matt made no reply, other than raising his hands to protect his face. "How did you find out?"

"Fredrick," Matt whimpered.

"Ugh," Steven growled shoving Matt back onto the floor. "Wait here, I have an arrest to make, when I return maybe I'll have calmed down enough to not want to kill you." With that, he locked Matt in the cell with Andrew and left. Immediately the silence got awkward.

"Are you okay Matt?" A small voice, from another cell, whispered into the darkness.

"What the flogging? I'm fine, it wasn't that bad," Matt answered, although he sounded worried.

"You betrayed our Father so I didn't have too," Andrew gasped in disbelief.

"I already have a thousand sins against him. What's a thousand and one?" Matt asked. "I couldn't let you take the fall though."

"I'm sorry I got you involved," Andrew asked him.

"It's sort of my fault," Matt muttered, but Andrew couldn't figure out what that meant. "Your ribs are broken, aren't they?"

"Only a couple," Andrew shrugged. "How can you tell?" Matt's shadow didn't answer but slowly crawled over to him, and a cold shaking hand touched his ribcage. Andrew tried not make any noise as he gently pushed in various parts. Finally he took his hand away and sat a few feet away.

"You're breathing, and I could be wrong, but four, possibly five, isn't a couple. It's also serious, with that many broken ribs you're at high risk of lung damage," Matt told him.

"I'm never going to see my wife or children again, am I?" Andrew whispered. Matt groaned as if he dealt with this every day and he was getting annoyed with it. He crawled back over to Andrew and literally ripped his shirt off from the collar bone all the way down his shackled arm. Matt must've been really good at doing that, cause he inflicted absolutely no pain before ordering him to take his shirt off. Andrew caused himself pain though, and it was difficult, but he managed to get his shirt off.

"Sit up straight, and lift your arms up," Matt ordered. Andrew bit his lip till he drew blood, but obeyed, and Matt aligned his broken bones, then wrapped Andrew's now ragged shirt around his ribcage, and it instantly felt better. "Okay, now breath, and take as big of a breath as the pain will allow."

"I've already done that," Andrew argued.

"Do it again," Matt ordered. "You probably should be doing that multiple times a day, and coughing just as often. Right now, I need to check to make sure the cloth isn't too tight."

"Shhh!" Andrew ordered.

"Relax, I have special privileges, now breath," Matt ordered again. Andrew rolled his eyes and obeyed, a moment later David was half dragged half lead back and re chained to his cell. "Uh... good enough. Do that as often as possible, and cough regularly, got it?"

"Yes Matt." Andrew groaned.

"Don't give me that, I'm not the little kid who used to follow you around the house begging you to play tag anymore," Matt argued.

"No, you're just the untrained doctor who's trying to fix me," Andrew complained.

"Do you want me to double check and see how many ribs are broken?" Matt threatened. "And for the record, I have a lot more experience with broken ribs than you do."

"See? You'll always be my pesky little brother," Andrew smiled softly. "I bet you don't threaten the other prisoners."

"I do when they're bugging me," Matt laughed. "Although, now that you mention it, none of the other prisoners locked me outside in the middle of the night."

"I forgot about that, and I was seven!" Andrew defended himself. "Besides, it was only half an hour."

"I was four, and it was cold, and scary!" Matt replied, although Andrew could hear the smile in his voice.

"Well you already had your revenge, remember tattle tale?" Andrew reminded him.

"Yeah," Matt laughed. "Didn't Pa make you wait in the barn for an hour while he calmed down?"

"Yes, it was terrible!" Andrew complained. There was silence for a total of five seconds before Andrew spoke again. "I love you," it was probably really random, but he needed Matt to know that.

"I'm sorry," Matt muttered to the floor, there was silence for a moment then he spoke again. "I can't believe you were harbouring a runaway slave."

"I wasn't, I was harbouring his stolen horse," Andrew answered. "The runaway slave went to Pa."

"I noticed." Matt shrugged. "Mind explaining how that arrangement worked out?"

"I didn't want Pa to have them both, so I took the horse, cause I figured that would lessen his danger for a bit, and it wouldn't be too risky for me."

"How did that work out for you?" Matt groaned.

"Well… not as well as I had hoped," Andrew explained. "What about you? How did running away from your problems work?"

"Not as well as I had hoped?" Matt answered with an unamused laugh.

"Fredrick told you Pa was helping him? That's the slave's name right?" Andrew answered.

"I sort of tricked him into telling me. As soon as I found out you were involved I figured it was either our family or Martha's. When we were alone I just told him, and I quote, 'My name is Mathew Couring, after my father. Most everyone calls me Matt, though.' The look on his face gave away where he was staying better than any words would've," Matt explained. "His master's planning to take him back to his property to whip him to death in front of the rest of his slaves, as soon as the trial is over though."

"I did not need to know that last part," Andrew groaned.

"Don't worry about it," Matt ordered. "He said ten months of physical freedom gave him eternity of spiritual freedom."

"What exactly do you do down here?" Andrew asked after a pause.

"I'm like the closest thing to a doctor the second level prisoners get. Speaking of which, I have to go, I have a hundred patients, and you just make a hundred and one, not to mention I have to clean about twice that many cells." Matt answered. For a minute Andrew thought he forgot the cell door was locked but he pulled out a set of keys and unlocked the door, stepped out, and locked it again. "Don't look at me like that, it's not like I have the keys to the handcuffs. Are you okay David?"

"Yeah I'm fine," David answered in a voice that sounded like he was trying to convince himself.

"Uh-huh... I'll get water to wash down your back," Matt told him. "George how's your arm doing?"

"It's fine, it's still immobilized remember?" Another prisoner, evidently George answered.

"Yeah I guess, I'll check your splint later if I have time, anyone else hurt or sick?" Matt asked.

"Who's going to wash your back?" Someone asked, Andrew was pretty sure it was the same person who objected halfway through Matt's flogging.

"Thank-you for your concern William, I'll see to it if I have time," Matt answered.

"MATT!" A chorus of prisoners objected in unison.

"Fine, I'll deal with it," Matt half laughed. "Seriously though, is anyone else hurt? Okay, I'll be back in a minute for you David."

"You two are brothers?" David asked when Matt was gone.

"I may not have known Matt had an older brother but I'm not surprised," William commented. "I mean, you said so yourself, he's probably the most decent person down here, and Matt is the only person whose job is to take care of us, and actually does it."

"What about the other ones?" Andrew whispered.

"The other four are lazy and selfish, they do the absolute minimum, and nobody really cares. Matt usually goes above and beyond," George told him.

"My brother Matt? The one that just came in?" Andrew demanded.

"That's the one," Someone else, whose name Andrew didn't remember, laughed. Andrew lay down on the cold stone floor, planning to wait until Mat got back, but passed out instead.

"Andrew wake up," Steven's voice ordered. Andrew nearly leaped to his feet, followed by a groan, and looked over at Steven who his Father in handcuffs. Mathew was staring at Matt, who looked like he was very reluctantly following. "Family reunion at it finest. In a jail cell. New punishment: instead of beating you Matt, I'm just going to make you tell your Father and brother what you've been up too this past year."

"I think I'd rather be beaten," Matt muttered.

"I know, that's why this is so perfect," Steven laughed. "If you refuse, you'll just be beaten, and forced to tell them. Not to mention the prisoners will finally see the real you, without the perfect mask."

"If he doesn't want to tell us..." Mathew interceded before being shoved onto the ground. Even with broken ribs Andrew was ready to take Steven on if only he could be released from his chains.

"I went on a travelling caravan, I was travelling for six months. It was fun, for a while I felt like I didn't have any problems. I had friends that I could hang out with during the day, I got to see tons of cool new places, and every night we'd sit around the campfire and party, so I never had to think about anything, I was busy all day, and drunk all night, it was perfect. The more I drank, the more it took to get drunk, but I thrived on it," Matt answered. "When I got back, I realized I was hooked, if I went to long without drinking, I'd start shaking and getting the worst pain. My life became all about when I'd get to be drunk next. I spent all my money, slept on the streets, skipped meals, begged, stole, anything to get the next bottle. Even then, I got into debt from drinking too much, and apparently when I was drunk I used to spend money on prostitutes, don't remember that part, but it diffidently got me into debt faster. Eventually the bar tender refused to give me anything until my tab was settled, I didn't know what else to do so I sold myself into slavery."

"You should've seen him the first few days he got here, he lay in the barn for days shaking and throwing up, it was quite the sight," Steven snickered, and Andrew suddenly realized he had never had that much hate for one person before in his whole life then he did for Steven. How dare he find his brother's pain amusing? "Anyway, why didn't you just go home, and ask your family for help?

"Cause I didn't want to face them," Matt muttered. "I didn't want to face my perfect family with an alcohol problem, and a debt that I would never be able to pay back. I sold myself into slavery 'cause I didn't wanna you to know how much I tarnished your good name," Matt answered.

"Alright," Steven announced before either Andrew or Mathew had a chance to say a word. "Mathew and Andrew your trial will be tomorrow, Mathew you're going to another section of second level. Matt, I'd get back to work, there's a boy in the west wing, and probably won't make it through the night."

"Wait!" Mathew objected but Steven silenced him, and forced him out of the room.

# CHAPTER 13

Matt sank to the ground next to Fredrick and wrapped some scrap rags around Fredrick fractured rib to help with the pain, and drenched a corner of his own sleeve in water to wash off all the dried blood from his face. Steven was busy giving Jason an overview of everything that had happened since Steven first dragged Matt down to Andrew's cell. Matt just tried to focus on Fredrick's wounds so he could get the look of his Father's face out of his mind.

"So anyway, after that interesting display of selfless love between brothers, I decided the best punishment would be to make Matt break his Father heart. I think it was better than a beating could have been 'cause I've never seen Matt cry before. It was amusing," Steven finished.

"That's really mean," Jason laughed. "Regardless, Fredrick! You told Matt but you wouldn't tell anyone else?"

"Matt figured it out," Fredrick answered raising his chained wrists in defence.

"Clearly you weren't hiding it very well," Jason argued. Fredrick just grinned, in such a way that Steven would probably kill Matt if he even thought about looking at him like that. Jason growled in exasperation and kicked his shin, but Fredrick didn't even appear to feel it. "I'm going to enjoy killing you."

"I'm going to enjoy dying," Fredrick told him. Jason didn't seem to know how to reply to that so he ignored it.

"Matt, it's time to go saddle the horses," Steven ordered.

"You need to help him," Jason ordered unlocking the chains and re clasping them around Fredrick's ankles. "You should feel great after Matt babied you, put a shirt on and stop being so sassy."

Once they got on ground level, and Fredrick somehow managed not to fall down the stairs, the first thing Fredrick said to him was: "Your Father still loves you Matt, it doesn't matter what you say to him."

"I know, that's the worst part. It's that I spat in his face and he still loves me," Matt sighed.

"What exactly did he make you say?" Fredrick asked hooking a lead rope to one of the horses.

"Everything I messed up this past year, and everything I did to avoid going home," Matt sighed resting his forehead on the other horse's forehead for a moment before hooking the harness on it. "You should've seen the look on his face."

Fredrick sighed and tried to lead the horse out but it wouldn't follow him. Matt watched for a moment before taking the lead rope from him.

"He's scared of your chains. Don't move and I'll take them both outside, then you can help," Matt suggested leading the timid horse out.

The two of them worked in silence for a while, other than Fredrick's chains rattling with every step, and Matt's occasional order to stop moving so he could get the horses calmed down. Thanks to that, it probably would've been faster if Matt had just done it himself. Still, Fredrick was grateful to not be chained to the bed.

"What makes you so sure he doesn't hate me?" Matt asked to fill the silence.

"You're his son, he loves you. I don't know, whenever he talked about you... I just knew. There really wasn't a doubt in my mind that he his love for you ever wavered," Fredrick shrugged. He sighed and rested on the edge of the carriage as Matt petted the skittish horse, silently praying Mathew and Andrew were going to be okay.

\*\*\*

Elizabeth sat down by the Oasis and stared at the trees around the pool. Matt and Andrew used to climb those trees, with their annoying little sister trying to follow them up. Her giant brothers, looking even bigger from the trees would look down at her struggling to climb up in annoyance. One scene, that must've happened when she was five, Matt seven, and Andrew ten, she still remembered like it was yesterday.

"*Come on Lizzie!*" *Matt groaned.* "*Can you be any more of a girl?*"

"*The branches are too high for me to reach! You two have longer legs then me!*" *Elizabeth yelled.*

"*Can't you play house by the water?*" *Andrew called back.*

"*I want to play with you!*" *Elizabeth answered. Matt and Andrew exchanged annoyed glances and finally Andrew hopped down to help her up. Satisfied she sat down on the branch beside Matt as Andrew climbed up a little higher and hung upside down to talk to his little siblings.*

"*So, what are we playing?*" *Elizabeth asked sitting with one leg on either side of the branch, which probably wasn't very ladylike, but that was how Matt was sitting, and she wanted to be like him.*

"*We're not really playing anything,*" *Andrew answered, his hair looking weird from being upside down.* "*We were just talking.*"

"*That's boring,*" *Elizabeth complained.*

"*Well what do you want to play?*" *Matt asked.*

"*Babies!*" *Elizabeth suggested.*

"*No,*" *both boys said in unison.*

"*How about we have a sword fight?*" *Matt asked.*

"*Elizabeth would die, literally,*" *Andrew pointed out.*

"*I can be a princess,*" *Elizabeth suggested.*

"*I guess that would work, Matt and I can fight over who gets the princess.*" *Andrew shrugged. So that's what they did. Both boys got sticks and 'sword fought' Andrew won of course, because he had a good three and half years on Matt, but then Matt stole the princess and took her too his lair, which just so happened to be bushes that they could both fit perfectly in, so Andrew had to fight for the princess again, which he won, again. They played all afternoon until Pa came out to get them for supper.*

*"What are you boys doing?" he asked, in answer Elizabeth ran into his arms and he swung her up above his head.*

*"Matt and Andrew are knights, and they're fighting over who gets the princess," she explained.*

*"Hey boys, she's my princess," Mathew argued. Andrew and Matt glanced at each other with mischievous sparkles in their eyes, and they fought Father pretty much as soon as he found a stick. That ended with Matt upside down and laughing in his Father's arms, and Andrew in a headlock. After Pa released them right side up and sent them the house for supper and scooped his princess up.*

*"And you." He laughed. "Are my fairest maiden in all the land."*

*"What's that mean?" Elizabeth asked.*

*"It means you're the prettiest princess in the whole world."*

Elizabeth stared at the spot where the big fight for her honour had taken place. It was there that Johnny had lay countless times staring at the sky, he never said why, even when he was asked, but hours he would stare at it. It was pretty close to that spot her and Fredrick had had that talk on Johnny's would be birthday and the one year anniversary of Matt's disappearance. It had looked so big when she was little, now, Elizabeth realized, it was small, more than that, it was empty.

"Elizabeth?" a voice called and she flipped her head around as Martha sat down next to her, with Jonathan on her lap. "What are you thinking?"

"Where's Mary-Liz?" Elizabeth demanded.

"That's not what you're thinking," Martha answered. "And she's with you Ma."

"Then why is Jonathan here?" Elizabeth sighed.

"Because Mary-Liz is two and a half, and Jonathan is six months," Martha answered. "How are you doing?"

"I'm fine," Elizabeth answered. "And I don't know, a lot has happened in the past few weeks."

"Yeah, I know, do you wanna talk?" Martha offered, Elizabeth just shook her head. "You can't carry everything forever Eliz."

"I can try," She argued.

***

"Andrew say something," David whispered from the other cell. Andrew heard him, but pretended to be asleep, in hopes that he would leave him alone. "Andrew!" Giving in, he softly moaned to let David know that he was still alive, not that there was any chance he'd miss it, his laboured breathing was probably reaching David's ears loud and clear. "Say something!"

"Hi," Andrew said, but even to his own ears he sounded strangled and oxygen deprived.

"Breathe," David ordered. "Take a deep breath, now." Andrew tried, honestly, but it turned into a bunch of painful, deep chest coughs that brought up a ton of thick phlegm. Actually whatever that was that he coughed onto his hand was two dark to be phlegm. He briefly panicked before realizing that it was too thick to be blood either, and settled back to being confused.

"They have to make an exception for him can't they? He was tortured!" someone Andrew didn't recognize complained.

"Andrew," David objected. "I know it hurts, but you need to try again."

"It's too late David," the first voice interjected. "Just leave him be."

"One: He still needs to breathe, it can get worse you know. Second: I'm not going to let another person die down here," David argued, a little too loudly and he was shushed by several prisoners.

For a while, there was no sound other than Andrew's laboured breaths.

"Andrew," David whispered again after a long time. Andrew moaned softly in answer. "Think about your family. They're what get you through."

"My soul... waits in silence... for God only..." Andrew contradicted, so short of breath as he quoted from Psalms 62, that he couldn't even talk properly, nor was he sure David could hear him. On the bright side, he knew for sure that the guard couldn't hear him. "From him... is my salvation... He only is my... rock and my salvation... my stronghold... I shall not... be greatly shaken."

"I see the family resemblance now," Someone commented beside him.

"Do you know that whole Psalm?" David asked.

"Yeah," Andrew gasped. "Me, Matt, and our... sister Eliz... Elizabeth... memorized... it together."

"Matt taught us up to verse eight," David told him. "My soul waits in silence for God only, from him is my salvation. He only is my rock and my salvation, my stronghold; I shall not be greatly shaken.

How long will you assail a man? That you may murder him, all of you, like a leaning wall, like a tottering fence? They have counseled only to thrust him down from his high position; they delight in falsehood; they bless with their mouth, but inwardly they curse

"'My soul, wait in silence for God only, for my hope is from him. He only is my rock and my salvation, my stronghold; I shall not be shaken. On God my salvation and my glory rest; the rock of my strength, my refuge is in God. Trust in him at all times, O people; pour out your heart before Him; God is a refuge for us.'"

"I like the other one Matt taught us, Psalms 121," George, the guy with the broken arm, commented. "I don't know remember the whole thing, but it starts off like 'I will lift up my eyes to the mountains; from where shall my help come from? My help comes from the Lord, who made heaven and earth."

"' He will not allow your foot to slip; He who keeps you will not slumber,'" David continued, and George joined in.

"Behold, He who keeps Israel will neither stumble not sleep. The Lord is your keeper, The Lord is your shade on your right hand. The sun will not smite you by day, nor the moon by night. The Lord will protect you from all evil; He will keep your soul. The Lord will guard you're going out and you're coming in from this time forth and forever."

Andrew smiled softly, though he knew no one could see him. He could hear chains rustling in various cells, but the only sound coming from Andrew's cell was painful, laboured breathing, and extremely painful coughing. He couldn't even tell when he slept and when he woke up, half an hour could have passed, or five hours, he was immune to time.

He couldn't help but wonder what had happened to Matt though, that would change him from a grieving little boy who ran away, to a strong Christian man that all these people looked up to, who taught criminals scripture verses to quote to each other in their cells. The supposed drunkard, who was now apparently the only one to take caring for the abused prisoners seriously. Whether it was because the prisoners already knew about the drunken adultery or not, they sure didn't care one way or another. Course, odds were they probably had done way worse things.

Finally the guard opened the cell door and walked in. "It's time for your trial," He announced. He held a blinding lantern up to his face, immediately Andrew moaned and closed his eyes. "You sound awful." Against his will Andrew was pulled into a sitting position and Matt's makeshift cast was untied. Instantly, the pain got worse.

"Put your shirt back on," the guard ordered unclasping the chain around his wrist. "I know it hurts but cloth around your ribcage like that isn't helping your breathing. If it weren't for the pneumonia I'd say leave it on, but like I always say, drastic times call for drastic measures. Stand up, good grief, how many ribs do you have broken anyway? Do you know?" the guard asked pulling him to his feet and cuffing his hands behind his back, the pain almost causing Andrew to pass out.

"Four... or five," he muttered.

"Well, here's hoping your trial goes in your favour..." the guard muttered before roughly leading him away.

# CHAPTER 14

The sight of his oldest son probably would've caused Mathew to throw up if he had anything in his stomach. If it was only him that had had to pay he would have nothing to regret, but he should never have let Andrew take that horse. They were still a distance away from each other, so Mathew couldn't hear him, but maybe it was because of all the times he had held Johnny has he gasped for air in his arms that could tell Andrew couldn't breathe just by looking at him. The guard seemed gentler with him then he was with Mathew when he shoved him into the prison waggon, but it was still too rough in his fatherly opinion. He silently cursed the chains immobilizing his hands behind his back that prevented him from doing anything. His son lay on the ground, almost sounding like he was trying to suppress the gasps for air.

"Andrew, are you okay?" Mathew asked. Andrew groaned in answer.

"You sound like Johnny," Matthew sighed.

"Not encouraging," Andrew reprimanded.

"You should sit up Andrew, struggling lungs don't like to lay down," Mathew told him. "And stop trying to talk, let your lungs have a chance to breath." Andrew let out a couple moans as he struggled into a sitting position and leaned against the wall. There was silence for a while, other than Andrew's random moan of pain as the carriage hit a bump.

"Please talk... to me..." Andrew whispered.

"I'm sorry, I shouldn't have let you take that horse, and I should have cancelled that get together. In the very least I should have asked if we couldn't come over to your house. I'm sorry I got you involved," Mathew sighed.

"I didn't ask... for the horse... I took it... remember?" Andrew gasped.

"When you were a little kid you used to cry when your siblings or your friends got hurt," Mathew sighed.

"I re...member," Andrew answered before breaking into a coughing fit that shook his whole ribcage and left him shaking with pain. Mathew winced in sympathy, staring at the dark green mucus that could only mean he had pneumonia.

"You have the biggest heart of anyone I've ever met, and your faith is so strong," Mathew continued, as soon as Andrew was done coughing, deciding that if he just kept talking Andrew wouldn't have chance to talk, and could focus on breathing. "I remember when you first accepted Jesus. You were five years old, and I was reading the bible, back then we used to do family devotions in the evening. Elizabeth was already asleep in your Ma's arms, and Matt was playing in the corner. It was just you three back then. Usually we had trouble getting you to listen, 'cause you always wanted to play with Matt, but that day you were wide eyed and listening. We took half an hour to read one chapter 'cause you kept interrupting and asking questions. Ma and I didn't care, we just answered your questions. They were hard questions too."

"Just wait, your day will come too, in a little more than two years I believe. Five-year-olds ask a thousand questions a day, and there are a few of them that are actually really good questions. Especially when they ask about the bible, and that day was no exception.

"Heaven was the theme, or to the five year old, it was living forever with Jesus, in a place where no one gets hurt, no one ever cries, 'cause there isn't anything to cry about, and no one is ever mean to anyone else. You were fascinated. Finally you asked how to get there. I told you that if you asked Jesus into your heart he would take you there when you die. I asked you if you wanted to ask him to come into your heart and you eagerly said yes. I taught you how to say the sinner's pray, and you said it. Your Ma and I, well in our minds it was the best day ever. You didn't totally understand everything that you did though, but you would. I remember when you were twelve, you started asking questions. Ma and I could do nothing but pray, we knew you had to find God for yourself, and you did. You were what? Fourteen?"

"Fifteen," Andrew corrected, his eyes so glazed Mathew was surprised he was actually listening.

"Right, I remember now. Even before then though, you had this amazing childlike faith. Now, I can honestly say your faith has humbled me. It's what defines you, it's your biggest passion," Mathew told him. Just then they hit a bump and Andrew moaned. Mathew sighed and kept talking. "I don't know what to say really. I'm sorry I got you into this mess. I should be the one lying on the ground in misery. I don't regret what I did though, I regret letting you be a part of it. I love you Andrew, and I'm so proud of you." As soon as he was done Andrew had another coughing fit, and Mathew reached out to hold his son before being stopped by the handcuffs behind his back.

"David thinks... I'm gonna die," Andrew gasped.

"Who's David?" Mathew asked.

"Am I... gonna die?" Andrew demanded.

"I don't know Andrew." Mathew sighed.

"I want to hold... Martha again... and the kids... and Martha's pregnant... I wanna meet..."

"Then meet the baby," Mathew interrupted. "Hold your wife and kids again. Paul says in Philippians 1:21-26 'For to me, to live is Christ, but to die is gain. But if I live in the flesh this will mean fruit from my labour, yet which I shall choose I cannot decide. For I am hard pressed between the two, having a desire to depart and be with Christ, which is far better. Nevertheless to remain in the flesh is more needful to you. And being confident of this I know that I shall remain and continue with you all for you progress and joy of faith, that your rejoicing for me may be more abundant in Jesus Christ be my coming to you again.' From your perspective, dying is a way better option, but you're so young and you have so much life ahead of you. God may still have plans for you."

"Thanks," Andrew whispered into the dim light, which seemed bright after the prison. There was silence again, and neither said another word until the prison carriage lurched to a stop and Andrew moaned miserably. A minute later the door was opened, two guards came to lead them into a courthouse.

For Mathew the trial ran in a blur. He remembered pleading for his dying son, in the end Mathew got five years, first month second level the rest on the first level. Andrew was released on the basis that he was going to die anyway.

***

Martha and Victoria had let Aaron come, but they made Ethel and Elizabeth stay with the children. Andrew was so weak Martha and Aaron half carried him, half dragged him to the carriage. He kept groaning, and Victoria couldn't even watch.

"Please I can't... get in the... carriage," Andrew complained.

"Andrew you can't walk," Martha told him gently, the sound of his voice making her heart break even more. She had seen him try to talk, but she couldn't hear him, he was too quiet. Now that she could hear his voice she wanted to break down and sob. "You have to try."

"I'll get the stairs okay? Then you can lay down in the back," Aaron told him.

"No," Victoria interjected. "Get the stairs, but he can sit up. It'll help him breathe."

"How did you get in the prison waggon?" Martha asked.

"A lot of pain," Andrew muttered. "And it was... lower."

"Alright, well you can try. I'll be right here to help you, remember Drew?" Martha reminded him. "Till death do us part?" Andrew didn't say anything, the poor guy was exhausted, but he smiled softly.

"Alright Andrew, that's the best we can do," Aaron announced setting the stairs down. "Do you want both me and Martha to steady you or just Martha?" Andrew just shrugged, so Aaron climbed into the carriage and pulled him up by the hand, as Martha made sure he didn't fall over. With a groan Andrew got into the carriage and sat in the back, leaning against the back.

For a moment the three of them just stared at him, the judge's words ringing in Martha's ears, and likely Victoria's and Aaron's as well. "Give Mathew a month in level two, five years altogether. As for Andrew, whatever. Release him, it's not like he's going to live a week anyway." As quick as it came the moment was over and Aaron sat down beside Victoria to drive, Martha beside Andrew in the back.

"Are we... going home?" Andrew gasped. He was so quiet Martha had to practically lean in to listen.

"No," She whispered playing with his fingers. "Soon though. Elizabeth had a panic attack and shut down, and I was getting overwhelmed with all the housework, cooking, and added list of barn chores, and Aaron was stressing out and looking for something to do, so we moved into your parents' house, we can move back though."

"I'm not gonna... be able to help... in the barn," Andrew reminded her. "And I need extra... help with... *everything.*"

"I know, I wouldn't expect you to be anything more than sick, but if you wanna go home we can move back, tomorrow at the earliest, it won't be that bad," Martha answered. Andrew gazed at her for a moment in a way he hadn't looked at her since they were courting before kissing her cheek.

"I miss... your smell," Andrew told her.

"My smell? I have a certain smell?" Martha asked, in answer Andrew grinned softly and nodded. "Thank-you, I missed you too."

They rode in silence for a bit before Martha changed the subject. "Do you know what's wrong with you?"

"Broken ribs I don't.... know what else... I could breathe... yesterday," Andrew answered.

"Victoria," Martha spoke up. "His ribs are broken, but that wouldn't cause this would it?"

"Um, he could have damaged his lungs when the ribs broke," Victoria answered crawling to the back of the waggon. "How many of your ribs are broken honey?"

"Four... or five," Andrew muttered, and Martha and Victoria exchanged glances.

"With that many broken, he could have easily damaged them after as well. If that's the case, there's nothing really we can do for him," Victoria explained.

*No wonder the judge decided he wouldn't live a week,* Martha thought sadly. Just then Andrew broke into a massive coughing fit that caused both Martha and Victoria to cringe with pain. Each cough was a deep congested cough that probably did not make his broken ribs feel good at all, and he was coughing up some weird, dark green mucous.

"Pneumonia," Victoria announced looking at the mucous. "I've heard that untreated broken ribs can turn into pneumonia, and that is diffidently pneumonia."

"So his lungs aren't damaged?" Martha asked.

"They might be, but pneumonia would make it hard to breath, and it's likely he's in so much pain he's trying to suppress the gasps for air, which would make him even shorter on oxygen," Victoria explained. "So damaged lungs or not, he's in rough shape." As if to prove her point Andrew coughed again, moaned in misery, and rested his head on Martha's shoulder. Victoria gazed at her son for a moment before burying her head in her hands.

"Matt," Andrew exclaimed half an hour later. "He told me to cough... and breathe deeply... but I didn't listen... that's why I can't... breathe... it was so cold... and..."

"Who's Matt?" Aaron interrupted.

"Our brother," Andrew answered, even breathless he sounded like that should be obvious.

"Matt ran away over a year ago, what are you talking about?" Aaron demanded.

"He's in... the prison," Andrew explained.

"What did he do?" Aaron asked.

"He didn't.... he's not a prisoner... he's a slave, he takes... care of the prisoners," Andrew explained.

"What do you mean?" Martha asked.

"The second level of a prison is the worst, and usually the only people to take care of the prisoners are slaves, who aren't trained except in the absolute basics, and are only required to feed and care for the prisoners enough to keep them alive," Aaron explained.

"Aaron, your father is in there, I don't want to hear about it," Victoria ordered

"Matt's different though," Andrew whispered. "The other prisoners... said he goes... above and beyond... what he's required to do... He even taught them... whole passages... of scripture... to quote to themselves, and each other."

"So, do you wanna fill in the blanks?" Victoria asked. "How did he go from a depressed runaway who wasn't living really, to a slave, who does more then he's required?"

"Drinking debt," Andrew answered. "And apparently... he discovered... that working nonstop... doesn't give you enough... time to think about... your problems. I don't know... the rest."

"Drinking debt?" Martha repeated.

"He said it killed... the pain," Andrew whispered.

"I'm so confused!" Martha complained.

"He belongs to the... head prison guard," Andrew explained. "The guy who... tortured me."

"Andrew, don't tell your Mother that!" Martha reprimanded.

"Well Matt seemed... to be in better... shape than the prisoners," Andrew shrugged. There was a long pause, while each person was lost in their own thoughts, and Martha drew circles on Andrew's calloused, weak hand.

"He said that Fredrick... the slave... was gonna be... whipped to death," Andrew whispered softly, so that only Martha could hear.

"Oh," Martha whispered. She thought briefly that she should say something else, but there was nothing else to say. Devastating was to normal a word to describe what that was.

"We have to buy... his freedom," Andrew told her.

"Slaves cost money, and that's something that we don't have," Martha lectured, still in a whisper. "Besides, did you even meet Fredrick? Not counting the time he was cowering in your brother's bedroom?"

"Matt did... and so did... everyone else," Andrew reminded her. "They loved him."

"I guess..." Martha began.

"I almost died... for him! He was half... dead," Andrew whispered. "His master... is cruel enough... to kill him. Slowly."

"We still don't have that kind of money, you need a doctor, you can't work, your Father is in prison, Matt's apparently a slave, I have two young kids, another on the way, and Aaron's exhausted. Where, pray tell, are you going to get that kind of money?" Martha demanded.

"The harvest money," Andrew told her.

"Andrew, that's all the money we have, possibly for a long time, we can't spend it all on one thing," Martha lectured again.

"Then get my ma... to help," Andrew ordered. "He's going to... kill him anyway... Fredrick can't be... expensive."

"Andrew, I don't know," Martha argued.

"Please Martha! No one... deserves... to be held... captive... and beaten... for every... minor... infraction. No one deserves... to be killed... for wanting... a better... life than that. Besides... I did not... go through... all that torture... for nothing," Andrew argued back. Martha sighed in defeat and flipped around.

"Andrew wants to buy Fredrick's freedom, but we don't have enough money to buy all of it, so he was wondering if we could work together," Martha spoke up.

"Yes," Aaron announced. "What made you decide this?"

"Aaron," Victoria reprimanded. "What about Matt?"

"Tell them." Andrew sighed.

"I can't Andrew, they've been through enough," Martha answered.

"Tell us what?" Victoria demanded in that voice Mother's got when they feared their children were in danger.

"Fredrick's master wants to whip him to death in front of the rest of his slaves," Martha blurted out. "He's taking him back right now."

# CHAPTER 15

Fredrick sank onto the dirt road watching Jason take care of last minute business. The chains around his wrists attaching him to the carriage were horrible reminders of his doomed existence. He wondered how long it would last before he would pass out, or would he pass out and Jason wake him up to endure more pain? Part of him was excited to go to heaven, the other part of him was terrified to die.

Just then a horse galloped up behind him and he flipped his head around to see, lo and behold, Aaron was there, riding on one the Couring's mare.

"What are you doing here?" Fredrick whispered angrily. Didn't he realize it was dangerous? Aaron ignored him and climbed down from the horse. He stood above him with his arms crossed looking down on him for a quarter of a minute.

"I don't know you, and you've never seen me before in your life, got it?" Aaron whispered, barely even moving his lips.

"Yeah," Fredrick whispered back, completely unsure what he was doing.

"Who's your master, boy?" Aaron asked, in a normal volume, and in a tone Fredrick had actually never heard out of his mouth before, his voice even changed. Fredrick couldn't speak if he wanted to, he just pointed to Jason. Completely in a new character Aaron walked, like a man with a purpose, over towards Jason and the two of them talked in the corner. Fredrick couldn't make out what they were saying, but he got enough to decide that if Aaron ever wanted to get into theatre he could make a lot of money. Finally the two of them walked over to Fredrick and Aaron studied him like a race horse he was interested in buying.

"Well, he is a hard worker," Jason shrugged. "And he's strong, feel his arms."

"I ran away," Fredrick added, hoping to bring his price down, plus, this whole thing was amusing. Both of them shot him a warning glance, one looking like he was trying not to kill him, the other looking like he was trying not to laugh.

"He's got a crush on one of my house slaves," Jason laughed. "He'll do anything not to be separated from her."

"I see," Aaron laughed as well, then he grabbed Fredrick's arm and pulled him to his feet. Aaron was a good actor, Fredrick actually felt like he was being sold to a man looking for a good slave. He stared at the ground as Aaron studied his face, pinched his arms, and felt his legs. Finally Aaron shrugged. "Well, he is strong, he can work in my fields. How much are you willing to sell him for?"

"Thirty dollars." Jason shrugged. From the sounds of how things went after that, it was Aaron's first time bargaining, but he managed to get him down to a somewhat decent price. They shook hands, signed some papers, and Aaron pulled out a bunch of money from his saddle bags. It all happened so fast, Jason unlocked Fredrick's chains, Aaron mounted his horse, and ordered Fredrick to walk beside him.

They actually made it out of the city before Aaron dismounted, sat in the sand, and as if waves of relief were washing over him. He even started laughing a bit, out of sheer relief.

"I'm alive," Fredrick gasped staring at the town they just left. "I'm alive."

"You're free, too, you know," Aaron told him. Fredrick collapsed onto the ground, which hurt his cracked rib, though he hardly noticed, and mentally ordered himself not to cry.

"I'm alive, I'm free, oh God I'm overwhelmed," Fredrick gasped.

"Well, I guess technically speaking, you belong to me, but we can fix that," Aaron shrugged.

"Where did that amazing acting come from?" Fredrick demanded.

"I don't know, Martha gave me this lecture about not letting him know who my Father or brother was, or even that I knew you, and that Jason couldn't know that I planned to free you, and it was probably best if he thought I was going to be mean. It actually wasn't that hard, I just pretended that was the truth," Aaron answered laying on the ground. "However, if he didn't make a joke after your 'I ran away' comment, my cover would've been blown!" Aaron argued, then tossed a handful of sand at Fredrick, and glared at him. "I missed you."

"I missed you too," Fredrick smiled softly. "How did you know where to find me?"

"Andrew," Aaron answered growing serious. "Apparently he found Matt, who told him where you were and that your Master wanted to make an example out of you. Andrew actually paid for half your freedom, since we didn't have enough on our own, and neither did he. He's not in good shape though, the judge actually released him 'cause he figured Andrew was going to die in a week anyway. He's at our house right now. Pa got five years though, the first month in second level."

"What's wrong with Andrew?" Fredrick demanded.

"He's got a like five broken ribs, and pneumonia. He's in a lot of pain, and he's not breathing very well," Aaron answered. "Come on, let's get back." Fredrick winced, the pain he was in, times five, with a lung infection? No wonder they thought Andrew was going to die!

They rode one in front of the other, and had barely dismounted when Fredrick was mauled by Elizabeth, Ethel, Laura, and Victoria all trying to hug him at once. Fredrick was so overjoyed to feel safe and loved for the first time since before his Father was robbed ten years ago, that he didn't even care that each hug cause rippling pain through his ribcage.

"Have you eaten anything?" Elizabeth asked, and Fredrick smiled.

"You're not going to try to stuff me to death again are you?" Fredrick demanded.

"Well, I'm just wondering," Elizabeth laughed back.

"Water, I'm good with water," Fredrick told her, as Laura hugged him again, fortunately not too hard.

"Nobody brushes my hair when you're gone," Laura told him.

"Nobody?" Fredrick smiled in mock outrage. "Well Elizabeth does better braids then me anyway."

"You're not that bad anymore, and she still doesn't brush it!" Laura complained. "Plus, there was no one to tell stories!"

"I think you got a little too used to me Laura," Fredrick laughed briefly before the pain ordered him to stop.

When they went inside though Fredrick almost lost it. How did this happen? He was safe and well. Free. One man that had mentored him and been like a Father to him was in prison so he could be free, and another man, that he had met once, was dying so he could live. Laura was hanging on his arm, refusing to let him go, and her Father was in a part of prison that didn't allow visitors.

Just then, a little girl about two or three peaked her head into the door and stared at him. He smiled at her to show that he wasn't scary but the little girl seemed to get more scared with that.

"Mama!" She objected. "There's a strange man in the kitchen!"

"It's okay sweetie, he's not going to hurt you," Victoria smiled assuredly. A moment later the girl who had come out to the fields with Elizabeth came out of the sitting room and swung her up onto her hip.

"That's Fredrick, don't worry, no one is going to take Papa away again," She explained, then offering him the hand that wasn't holding her daughter she added. "It is Fredrick right? I'm Martha, and this shy little thing is Mary-Liz."

"Nice to meet you," Fredrick answered, returning an awkward handshake since Laura was still hanging on his right hand.

"Here, as requested," Elizabeth announced handing him a cup of water, which Fredrick gratefully accepted and downed in one gulp.

"Thank you," he answered placing it on the counter.

"Do you want another one?" Elizabeth asked staring at the now empty cup. Fredrick nodded, and Elizabeth refilled it twice before Victoria cut him off.

"Did he give you anything to drink while you were there?" she demanded.

"No, I was going to die anyway, so he didn't bother to waste food or water on me," Fredrick answered.

"And then he expected you to keep up with a buggy in the desert sun?" Aaron demanded. Fredrick only shrugged.

"Well anyway, if you drink too much at one time it will all go straight through you, it's best if you have more later," Victoria answered.

"Yeah, I guess," Fredrick shrugged. "Is Andrew awake?"

"Yeah, he's in the sitting room right now, we're not going to attempt the stairs for a while," Martha answered.

Fredrick nodded and opened the door to the sitting room, Laura, not so surprisingly, still clinging to his hand. Fredrick had only met Andrew once, and the man sitting in the chair was exhausted, but Fredrick recognized him. A baby sat facing Andrew, on his lap, while Andrew gently tickled him so the baby was a fit of giggles. Still, the baby was far enough away so even when he leaned forward, he couldn't touch Andrew's ribcage, the trick seemed to be not letting him fall over backwards.

"Andrew?" Fredrick greeted softly. Andrew looked up at him and offered a tired smile. Fredrick slowly walked over to where Andrew sat and squatted in front of him, and Laura promptly sat down on his lap. "I'd say thanks, but it doesn't seem to be enough. You saved my life, and bought my freedom in the process, I don't even know you."

"I only paid... for half you're... freedom though," Andrew told him, he pointed to his wife still holding Mary-Liz in the corner. "She wouldn't let me... pay for all of it."

"I don't think I would've let you either," Fredrick smiled, hoping his surprise didn't show on his face. Aaron had said he was having trouble breathing, but Andrew couldn't even talk properly! "I owe my life to you, in more ways than one. You took the horse, bought my freedom, and who knows what happened to you in the prison, you sound awful by the way."

"The wounds... were more for... my Father," Andrew told him.

"They were trying to get you to say where I was staying," Fredrick nodded understandably. "You look like you got Steven too, only worse, because my master wouldn't let him torture me to much. He wanted me to live."

"Wasn't that bad... the lung... infection... came later..." Andrew answered.

"Yeah, I can see it wasn't that bad," Fredrick nodded sarcastically. "Well, I'll stop talking to you, so you can breathe, but I swear, if you ever need anything I'm available."

Andrew smiled and glanced past him to check that his wife and daughter were the only other ones in the room, and grinned mischievously. "Do you like Elizabeth?"

"You do," Laura laughed softly.

"No I don't," Fredrick argued.

"Then why are your cheeks red?" she teased.

"You guys she's in the other room," Fredrick reminded them covering his apparently red cheeks that were actually really warm.

"She can't... hear us," Andrew told him.

"Yeah, I highly doubt she can hear us." Martha giggled. "Andrew's too quiet, she likes you too, by the way."

"She does?" Fredrick demanded looking over at Martha, simultaneously Andrew and Laura nodded.

"It's kind of... obvious," Andrew told him.

"Well, I'll uh, let you relax and stop talking now," Fredrick answered, quickly leaving the room, Laura following behind as his new attachment. He could hear Andrew and Martha giggling to themselves as he left, though.

For most of the afternoon, he just enjoyed being home. He helped Elizabeth make supper, and even told a story when they all begged him too. Everyone gave him undivided attention, except Elizabeth, who cooked and listened at the same time. After supper he and Aaron went out to the barn where they took care of all the animals, new and old. Fredrick was collecting the last of the eggs and Aaron was wiping down the last horse when Elizabeth came in.

"How are you doing?" Fredrick asked.

"Okay." Elizabeth shrugged.

"Hey Aaron, do you wanna take in the milk and eggs? I can finish up in here," Fredrick offered.

"Yeah, sure, you two have a lot to talk about, try to be in before it's time for morning chores," He teased, although Fredrick suspected he was half serious.

Turns out, he was totally serious. Elizabeth may have tried to hold herself together for too long, 'cause she broke down and sobbed as soon as they were alone. It was almost five minutes before Fredrick even got her to say anything, he just held her in his arms while she drenched his shirt in tears.

"What's this?" She asked pulling away and feeling the cloth under his shirt.

"It's nothing, I'm fine," Fredrick told her. Elizabeth looked at him for a minute and pushed her palm right into his broken rib.

"You're broken, too!" Elizabeth accused when he grunted.

"Only once, it's not like Andrew, and I wasn't in a cold damp prison, you don't need to worry," Fredrick told her.

"Really?" Elizabeth demanded. Fredrick took a deep breath, which actually wasn't as deep as he could usually go before Elizabeth hit him, and nodded.

"Really, you worry too much," Fredrick told him. "Andrew is the most important patient, I just have an injury."

"You're too tough," Elizabeth lectured. "One of these days you're going to die!"

"You're lecturing me about being too tough?" Fredrick demanded. "What about you? I'm only physical, you bottle up everything else!"

"You were gone! I watched Andrew be arrested, then he came back like that. My Father is in prison, he's going to be there for years, even when I can talk to him again, it'll be through bars! Apparently everybody has been talking to Matt, who's like this Christian icon now, well why doesn't he come home and apologize if he's so perfect these days? And on top off all that, you were gone Fredrick, you're the only person I can talk to and you have the same injury as my dying brother does!" Elizabeth yelled.

"Elizabeth," Fredrick interrupted. He could be angry with just about anybody, he could handle just about anyone angry at him, but he couldn't handle Elizabeth. "I'm sorry, okay? I didn't think it was that important."

"That's because everyone taught you that you weren't important," Elizabeth snapped. "That's why you didn't say anything when it was your birthday, that's why you didn't say anything when your rib was broken, and who knows what else. Fredrick, you are important. To me, and to my family. I don't care if you don't believe it, I believe it. God believes it. Jeremiah 31:3b 'I have loved you with an everlasting love; therefore I have drawn you with lovingkindness.' John 15:9 'Just as the Father has loved Me, I have also loved you; abide in My love.' Don't you get that yet? It doesn't matter what man has labelled you as, you are loved with an everlasting love, understood?"

"Understood," Fredrick nodded, smiling slightly. "It's just… weird. Do you remember in Mathew 18:21-22? 'Then Peter came and said to Him, 'Lord, how often shall my brother sin against me and I forgive him? Up to seven times? Jesus said to him, 'I do not say to you, up to seven times, but up to seventy times seven times.' I want to forgive them."

"How? They arrested my father, tortured my brother, planned to kill you, are holding my other brother as a slave, and you think you can just forgive them?" Elizabeth demanded.

"Not on my own," Fredrick shrugged. "But the very one who wants me to forgive is there to help."

"I want to do what God wants, but I can't," Elizabeth grumbled.

"Do you think I can?" Fredrick half laughed. "I have the benefit of a whole year working on forgiveness, and fortunately God has a lot of grace. Jesus was tortured, arrested, and even killed for us, the least I can do is do what he says."

"I can try to forgive them too, but it's not going to be easy," Elizabeth shrugged.

"Of course it's not going to be easy," Fredrick nodded. "But in the words of your father, 'it's 'cause it's worth it.'"

# EPILOGUE

Matt leaned against the cold brick wall and took a deep breath, he had begged his Father in a voice that was barely above a whisper to save anything he wanted to say to him until he was up at first level. The cells there were more soundproof, if they talked in whispers nobody would over hear them, and they could make eye contact if needed thanks to the extra light.

For a month at least, Matt had put off that deep conversation with his Father, and hadn't even treated him any different then he treated the other prisoners, although it had seemed slightly more awkward when he washed his flogged back down. Now, he had to face him, and he couldn't put it off any longer. Before he could lose his nerve he unlocked Mathew's cell door and walked in.

"I bet this place feels like a five star hotel after second level," Matt commented coming in. Mathew looked up from where he lay staring at the roof, on the pile of hay, he was no doubt using as a bed, and nodded. "Hope you weren't sleeping. Have you had company yet?"

"Yeah, Andrew's still alive, he's literally in the middle of a life or death battle, but he's alive, which is a miracle in itself. Fredrick's free, which is also amazing. And they brought me bread, do you want some."

"I'm fine," Matt began before his father tossed him a quarter loaf anyway.

"Your too thin Matt, eat something. Besides, I already ate most of it. Do you have time?"

"Yeah, I'm done work for the day, it's bedtime but I thought I could put sleep off for a few more minutes," Matt shrugged, raising the bread to his nose and taking a deep breath. Sure enough it was Ma's bread. The scent filled him with a feeling of longing, regret and sadness. He sighed and lowered his voice before asking the question that he had wanted to ask all month, and had been terrified of the answer. "Do you hate me?"

"Why would I hate you?" Mathew asked. Matt didn't answer, his father had a thousand reasons to hate him. Finally Mathew sighed. "C'mere Matt, there is one thing I need to make totally and completely clear. My love for you is unconditional, if you runaway, become a drunkard, whatever, it may affect how I feel, but I still love you, simply because I love you, I love you today, the same as I loved you when the midwife first told me I had another son, and every day in between. There is nothing you can do, or anyone else can do that will make me love you anymore. There is nothing you or anyone else can do that will make me love you any less. I just love you."

"Are you disappointed in me?" Matt asked.

"That's a different question then 'do you hate me' and it depends on what we're talking about," Mathew admitted. "Those prisoners down there have hope because of you. I was one of them, I heard how they talk. I was only down there a month but some of them are down there for years. Those people have hope because of you, some of them even have faith in God because of you. Matt, your different, you're not the same person you were when you ran away. You used to be quite and scared, you stopped living even.

"About that, why did you runaway in the first place? What exactly was that supposed to accomplish?"

"I don't know," Matt sighed. "I was angry, and sunk in grief. That whole house seemed to be filled with reminders that Johnny wasn't there anymore. The bed that I slept in by myself, his empty chair. I couldn't take it anymore so I ran, I guess I thought I could outrun the pain."

"And how did that work out?" Mathew asked, sounding like he already knew the answer, he just wanted Matt to admit it.

"It didn't," Matt confessed. "Mostly it just suppressed the pain until it came back up again. And it did, a lot. I guess that was why I started drinking, it actually worked. But didn't solve anything, it just made me forget about it, and it caused more problems then made me forget anyway."

"So what happened that made the runaway drunk meet God?" Mathew asked, this time actually sounding curious.

"Well, I already told you I drank myself into debt, and to settle it I sold myself to the head prison guard," Matt answered. "The first few days were awful, I was in so much pain. I remember begging Steven for a drink, but he wouldn't let me have anything. He said he had no use for a drunken slave, and I was just going to have to get over it. He just left me in his stable, lying on a pile of hay, vomiting, with mind numbing cramps.

"When I could work, he got me to take care of the prisoners on first level, giving the prisoner's food, cleaning their chamber pots, you name it. Then he sent me to second level. It was literally the worst thing I had ever seen.

"I remember when I first went down there was this one prisoner, named Markus, supposedly he killed his own daughter but I don't know. I felt like everyone knew me as the alcoholic and I just wanted someone to love me for me, so I never really attached him to his sin, I just saw that both his legs were broken, and he sounded breathless when he talked. I've been down there enough to know his ribs were probably broken too, but I didn't know it at the time. I sat with him for hours, talking to him. I technically didn't have to, because he was going to die anyway, but I felt like I couldn't leave him.

"I told him about how Jesus was crucified for our sins, and about this thief on the cross who was crucified next to him that asked for forgiveness and Jesus told him 'today you will be with me in paradise' it's funny, because I didn't even think I was worthy of forgiveness, but here I was, telling a man, who had done way worse things, that Jesus could forgive him. He accepted Christ that day, when I was finished work that day I lay on a pile of hay that I call my bed, and cried. At first I was mad at God that he would let people live like that, regardless of what they had done, then I thought about how Markus had accepted Jesus. God had forgiven him, God had forgiven the thief on the cross, and sometimes God lets us suffer so we'll come to him. I accepted Christ that day too. The next day, I went down to second level again, and Markus was dead.

"I was devastated, but I refused to let myself sink into depression like when Johnny died. I told myself that I was going to live for both of them. That I was going to make the world a better place. You may have already picked this up from your month down there, but the slaves are only required to take care of the prisoners who could die if they aren't taken care of or they could have permanent damage. If they're guaranteed to die, you can leave them, and if they'll heal with time, it also doesn't matter either. I don't know, obviously those should be top priority, but then there are the people who die all alone, who can barely move from the pain and are ignored.

"God could forgive me, God could forgive the thief on the cross, and those prisoners down there needed to hear God. You said once that the best way to reach a man's spiritual needs is through his physical needs so that's what I did. I started cleaning their living spaces, washed their torn and tattered backs, aligned and bandaged their broken bones. Then I got to tell them about the faith that I myself only just started to understand. They comfort each other now, when I'm not there. I've caught them quoting the scripture I taught them to each other."

"Interesting." Mathew grinned softly. "That's wonderful Matt, I'm glad you know the Lord now."

"I wanted to come home, but I couldn't," Matt sighed playing with the loaf in his hands. "I can't exactly leave without running away again, and trust me, those few days with Fredrick cured me of any plans to escape. I'm sorry, it's not your fault. I don't know if you ever thought it was, but I was already planning to run away when we had that fight on Johnny's birthday. The fight made me decide to runaway three days early, but I already had a job with a travelling caravan by that time, and anyway, I knew I had a place to stay with people you didn't even know."

"You really put a lot of thought into that didn't you?" Mathew sighed, and Matt could only nod sheepishly. "No wonder we couldn't find you, how long did you work with the travelling caravan?"

"Six months," Matt shrugged. "Then I lived on the streets for four, and I've been a slave ever since. So I guess during those four months I could have come home, but I didn't."

"Matt, if you had come sooner you would just be in trouble for helping Fredrick," Mathew pointed out. "Besides, God has a habit of turning our mess ups into glory. Just let him."

"I guess," Matt shrugged.

"Matt, I'm not perfect," He sighed. "I'm guilty of shutting everybody out after Johnny died too. Sometimes I wonder if I had been more of a Father to you when you needed it, things would've ended differently."

"It might have, but I don't know if I would've let you in," Matt pointed out. "I think we both shut each other out. Johnny was adorable, and he was too young. Still, Elizabeth was the only one not guilty of shutting everyone else out. Ma retreated to her room, you to your work, and me... I don't even know where I went. I was so angry. I used to run to the tombs where he was buried, and lay down in the sand just screaming at God. Everything made me angry it seemed like. I ran away 'cause I wanted to get back at you, but honestly, to this day, I can't figure out what you did that made me need to get back at you. I guess I was just mad that our family was different. More than that, I was mad that nobody else seemed to notice it. You all were starting to heal, and I was still mad that he was gone, so I ran."

"I looked for you for months, after a few weeks I had to go back to taking care of the farm, but I still looked every moment I had. It wasn't until Fredrick showed up that I started to sleep at night. I use that term loosely, but it was better than before I guess. If your time line is accurate, I gave up halfway through your trip," Mathew sighed.

"I'm sorry," Matt muttered to the floor.

"Don't be, I'm telling you that this is my fault too," Mathew corrected. "I want you to know that I still love you. I worry about you, that's what I do. Your Ma, she was so worried, I was worried about her. She loves you too Matt." Matt didn't answer, mostly because he wasn't sure what to say to that.

"Go to sleep, I'll be here tomorrow." Mathew decided. "We have five years, at least, where we can work on building a friendship."

Matt smiled softly and played with the piece of bread in his hands. There was nothing else to say, but he slowly broke off a piece and popped it in his mouth. Maybe, just maybe, the bread didn't taste as bad as he thought it would.

# About the Author

Breanna is a young lady who has loved writing since grade two. She was homeschooled from grade five and wrote her first novel just for fun. Although this is the first book she has gotten published, she has always been a writer at heart.

She committed her life to the Lord a month before she turned sixteen and has a passion for seeing the church become an "army for the Lord."

She lives in a small town in southern Alberta, Canada, with her parents and younger brother and sister.

Printed in the United States
By Bookmasters